P9-COP-655

DAUGHTERS OF THE MOON

into the
cold fire

LYNNE EWING

VOLO

HYPERION/NEW YORK

Copyright © 2000 by Lynne Ewing
Volo and the Volo colophon are trademarks of Disney Enterprises, Inc.

First Edition
3 5 7 9 10 8 6 4 2
Printed in the United States of America

Library of Congress Cataloging-in-Publication Data
Ewing, Lynne.
Into the cold fire / Lynne Ewing.—1st ed.
p. cm. - (Daughters of the moon ; #2)
Summary: Serena, a moon goddess who has the special gift of reading minds, is torn
between joining the dark force of the evil Atrox and staying with her friends, the
Daughters of the Moon.
ISBN 0-7868-0654-0 (trade : hc)
[1. Supernatural—Fiction. 2. Los Angeles (Calif.)—Fiction.] I. Title.
PZ7.E965 In 2000
[Fic]—dc21   00-038481

Visit www.hyperionteens.com

For Laura Brooks,
meam mirabilem consobrinam

———～✦～———

Many thanks to Victor Carrillo, Jr.,
Angela Hayden, Nadia Marquez,
Julie Morales, Ivania Sandoval, and
Mike Terrell for sharing a small part of their
lives with me, and a special thank-you to my
wonderful editor, Alessandra Balzer.

◄

In antiquity, Hekate was loved and revered as the goddess of the dark moon. People looked to her as a guardian against unseen dangers and spiritual foes.

All was well until Persephone, the goddess of spring, was kidnapped by Hades and ordered to live in the underworld for three months each year. Persephone was afraid to make the journey down to the land of the dead alone, so year after year Hekate lovingly guided her through the dark passageway and back. Over time Hekate became known as Persephone's attendant. But because Persephone was also the queen of the lower world, who ruled over the dead with her husband, Hades, Hekate's role as a guardian goddess soon became twisted and distorted until she was known as the evil witch goddess who stalked the night, looking for innocent people to bewitch and carry off to the under-world.

Today few know the great goddess Hekate. Those who do are blessed with her compassion for a soul lost in a realm of evil. Some are given a key.

CHAPTER ONE

SERENA KILLINGSWORTH stood on the shoulder of Pacific Coast Highway near the bluffs, waiting for her surf-rat brother to pull his surfboard from the back of the utility van. She stared out at the gray-green water and breathed in the briny smell of sea and kelp. Overhead seagulls circled with their shuddering *kee-yah*s.

"Awesome," Collin said behind her. "The waves are really pumped up."

Her thoughts had been on something more deadly than surf. Still she smiled when she turned to her brother. "Great set," she agreed.

Collin pulled his wet suit from the back of the van and snapped it into place. He was such a board-head that he ignored warnings about surfing alone, especially at night. Serena didn't question his swimming. He was strong. It wasn't riptides, sharks, or wipeouts that made her fear for his safety. She knew of other things that made a Los Angeles night perilous. And lately those dangers had become more menacing.

"Aren't you going out?" he asked, and motioned with his head to her board.

"No," she said, and tied her sweatshirt around her waist. She wore a long-sleeved bathing suit. She had planned to go out. But that was before something had happened at school. Now she needed time to think.

"Should," he said.

"I'll wait on the beach."

A wind blew at the incoming waves, holding them up and making them more hollow. Perfect for surfing.

"It's classic," he said. "You sure?"

"Sure."

The setting sun speckled his crystal-blue eyes with flecks of light and colored his long white-blond hair fiery gold. Nothing about the two of them looked similar. Her hair was dark, the roots almost black, the tips Crayola red. Pointy black shades hid her green eyes, and her tan was even darker than his because she loved the sun and hated the sticky feel of sunblock.

"So," Collin said, and pulled out his board. "How was school today?"

She stiffened.

"Well?" He threw down a towel and set his board on top.

She felt ambushed. "I guess you know already or you wouldn't be asking." There was no way he could know what had happened unless Morgan Page had told him. Morgan had a crush on Collin and used Serena as an excuse to talk to him.

"You're getting a flaky reputation," Collin warned. He grabbed a chunk of paraffin from the back of the van, got down on his knees, and started rubbing a thin layer of wax on the deck of the board.

Serena tried to swallow her anger. If he knew the facts, he wouldn't question her. She smiled to herself and fantasized about telling Collin what her true identity was. She imagined the surprised look on his face. Would he feel proud of her? Or frightened? For sure, he would never look at his younger sister the same way again.

"It's not funny," he said as if he could sense her smiling.

Her daydream slid away. "What did Morgan tell you?"

He stopped waxing the board and gazed up at her. A strange look crossed his face.

Immediately she realized she had made a mistake.

"I never said it was Morgan." Then his face relaxed and he chuckled, "You always know how to read my mind."

She breathed out. No need to panic this time. He'd gotten used to the way she sometimes knew what he was thinking. He thought it was because they had become so close after their mother left them. If he only knew.

"It was easy to guess," she said simply. "Morgan exaggerates so she'll have an excuse to call you."

He stood and threw the wax into the back of the van with a loud thump. "Did she say that?" A sly smile crept across his face.

"No," Serena responded. Then she caught the puppy-dog look in his eyes and whispered a quick prayer, *please, no*. Things were already difficult enough without adding Morgan to the mix. It would be a nightmare if Collin liked her. Serena had a mental flash of Morgan hanging out at their house, watching her, following her, nosing around her bedroom. It was bad enough she had to see her at school every day. Morgan seemed to suspect that something about Serena and her three best friends—Jimena, Catty, and Vanessa— was different. She had no idea how different they actually were. Still, some days she snooped disturbingly close to the truth.

She sighed. "You'd like to go out with her, wouldn't you?"

"No." He spoke too quickly. She didn't need to be a mind reader to know that was a lie.

"Yes, you would," she pointed out matter-of-factly.

"I'm just going to meet her for coffee." He took a thin plastic blade with a serrated edge and scored grooves into the wax on his board. "What's wrong with that?"

"She asked you to meet her to talk about me, didn't she? Like she wants to help."

"How do you know that?" He tossed the wax comb into the van and slammed the cargo door.

"I know Morgan. I thought you did, too. Did you forget? You always said she doesn't have boyfriends, she takes prisoners." Serena hated the nag in her voice.

"Morgan's changed." He was being annoyingly defensive.

"Not enough," Serena muttered and turned away. She couldn't tell Collin what had really happened to Morgan last month to make her change. He probably wouldn't believe her anyway. Even Morgan didn't understand what had actually been done to her. If she did, she would have been more frightened by those punks this afternoon. Morgan couldn't know how vulnerable she was right now. That was one reason Serena and Jimena had risked exposing themselves in order to protect her. Had Morgan seen them do anything strange this afternoon? She clicked her barbell tongue pierce nervously against her teeth.

Collin started to pick up his board but stopped. A look of astonishment crossed his face. Had she slipped? Given something away?

"What?" she asked.

"Your moon amulet." He reached for it. "It changed color."

She took a quick step back before he could touch it. She looked down at the amulet hanging around her neck and studied the face of the moon etched in the metal. The charm had been given to her at birth. It wasn't pure silver, but sparkling in the light of the setting sun, it cast back a rainbow of shimmering lights. Jimena, Catty, and Vanessa each had one, too. Serena never took hers off.

"Probably the setting sun." She clasped her

hand around it. The amulet resonated as if an electrical current passed through it. Did that mean one of them had followed her? She looked quickly behind her. Traffic continued down the highway, tires humming. She didn't see anything odd that should alert her to danger.

She wished Jimena were here. Normally, they were inseparable, but this evening Jimena had to do community service at Children's Hospital. She worked with children undergoing rehabilitation for gunshot wounds. She read to them, played checkers, and showed them how to macramé. Jimena had been in a gang and sentenced twice to a Youth Authority Camp for jacking cars. She would be there now, if a lenient judge hadn't sentenced her to do community service work instead. Jimena had been one badass homegirl before she understood her destiny. Their destiny.

Collin placed his hand on her shoulder.

Here it comes, she thought. She mouthed the words as he spoke behind her.

"I'm concerned about you. . . ."

But his next words took her completely by surprise.

"Maybe if you had a boyfriend—"

She spun around on him. *"What?"*

"Morgan says that's why you act the way you do . . . because you don't have a boyfriend. You never—"

"The last time I tried to have a boyfriend, you scared him away. You were always in his face." She couldn't tell him the real reason it was so difficult for her to have a boyfriend.

He shrugged it off. "You're older now. Maybe if you found someone—"

"A guy isn't the answer." Anger burned inside her. She was so annoyed at Morgan that she wanted to explode. But how could she be mad at Collin when she knew how much he worried about her?

Collin spoke softly now, sensing her anger. "She said she was flirting with these guys, and you and Jimena came up and started talking gibberish."

"It wasn't gibberish. It was Latin," Serena snapped, and immediately wished she hadn't.

"Latin?" Collin repeated in disbelief. "No one speaks Latin. It's a dead language." He looked at her curiously. "When did you learn Latin, anyway?"

"Just did." Again she wished she hadn't mentioned the Latin. It was one more secret. She had been born with the ability to speak Latin and ancient Greek. She just hadn't known it until she had learned about her destiny.

"Morgan said you were really upset. What did they say in *Latin* to get to you?"

She sighed. *"Foeda dea."*

"What does that mean?"

"Ugly goddess."

"Goddess?" He seemed to think that was funny. "That upset you?"

"Forget it." She started walking toward the beach.

"Morgan says kids at school call you the Queen of Bizarre."

She whirled around.

"Morgan," she corrected. "Only Morgan calls me the Queen of Bizarre. Everyone else likes me."

At least she thought they did. They seemed nice enough to her, all except Morgan, who seemed to have some personal vendetta against her that she didn't understand.

"Well, it's a little odd you made those guys get away from her," Collin said.

"It wasn't like Jimena and I didn't have a reason for doing what we did. But Morgan didn't tell you about that, did she?"

"What was it?"

"Those guys were bothering her. I don't know why she told you she was flirting with them. Morgan's never liked hard-core punkers. She likes jocks. She was telling them to get away from her and they wouldn't. I mean, the guys were wearing chains with padlocks and they each had five hoops piercing their lips."

Collin gave her an amused look.

"Okay, I've got piercings, but these guys have faces that look like pincushions, jailhouse tattoos for time spent, and a major attitude."

"Punkers who speak Latin?" He looked doubtful.

Why had she mentioned the Latin? "Yes."

"That's not how Morgan described it."

"Of course not," Serena said with frustration. "She wanted an excuse to call you and she couldn't tell you that Jimena and I rescued her, because then she might look bad. She's lucky Jimena and I were around." Morgan didn't know how lucky. She never had the best judgment about people. Then another thought came to her. What if Morgan had tried to set it up to see what she and Jimena would do? Could she know that much?

Collin smiled broadly. "So you and Jimena rescued Morgan? Chased the bad boys away?" He hugged her and she could smell the neoprene rubber of his wet suit. "Cool. My sister and Jimena Castillo, sophomore vigilantes of La Brea High."

That was closer to the truth.

"So don't worry about it," she said.

But he was already looking back at the ocean. The waves called. Morgan was forgotten.

"Let's go." He picked up his board and started walking.

They slipped through a narrow opening in a

fence. She took off her blue sandals and walked down the spongy ice plant that covered the sandy slope, then followed Collin to the shoreline. Sand squeezed through her toes. She kept glancing at her moon amulet. It was no longer glowing. She wondered what it had picked up earlier.

At the water's edge Collin slipped the Velcro strap around his ankle that leashed him to his surfboard. A wave fanned across the sand and Serena felt the cold water gather around her ankles with a shock.

"Damn," Collin muttered.

She looked at the sets rolling in. Two other surfers rode the waves. Collin liked time alone.

"Be careful," she said.

"No fear," he whispered. He hesitated a moment as if he were uttering a prayer to the great Kahuna, the only true surf god. Then he charged into the waves, slipped the board into the darkening water, slid on top, and paddled over the next wave.

She waited in the foam and backwash until he caught his first wave. The setting sun glowed through the wave and silhouetted him. He was phenomenal. Hanging ten was his specialty. It wasn't easy. To do the move he had to abandon the usual sideways stance that made it easier to control the board. He stood on the tip of the nose, all ten toes hanging over, knees slightly bent, arms balancing out to his sides. Sometimes crowds gathered and watched his nose-riding.

She walked along the wet sand over broken clam and cockle shells. The soft roar of surf and the constant hum of traffic on Pacific Coast Highway were a pleasant relief from the noise that usually filled her mind. The water rolled over her feet and the backwash pulled the sand beneath her steps back to the ocean.

She wished she could tell Collin the truth. She hated keeping so many secrets from him. If only he knew, then her behavior wouldn't seem strange. But would he believe her even if she did tell him she was a goddess, a Daughter of the Moon? And that she was here to protect people from the Atrox, an evil so ancient it had tempted Lucifer into his fall? He'd probably think she'd become a druggie or gone mental.

She glanced back at the waves. Collin caught another, then kicked off as the wave broke into frothy whitewater. What would he do if she did tell him? It wasn't as if she couldn't prove to him that what she said was true, because she also had a gift. She could read minds.

She hadn't understood her power when she was little. She only knew then that she was different from everyone else. Sometimes in the excitement of playing, she'd forget her friends weren't speaking and she'd answer their thoughts. Even now, if she became too happy or excited, she'd answer people's thoughts as if they had said them out loud. That was one reason it was difficult to have a boyfriend. It wasn't just Collin who had freaked out the last guy. She'd done a good job of that herself. She had been sitting in his car, listening to him say all these nice things about her. She had nodded her head and said *thank you* and *I like you, too.* Then she had looked at his face and known immediately from his puzzled expression that he hadn't uttered a word; she'd been answering his thoughts. It had definitely been bye-bye time after that. She had been too embarrassed to see him again. She still blushed whenever she saw him in the hallway at school.

She climbed over barnacle-covered rocks exposed by the low tide and walked around a pile of yellow-brown kelp. The seaweed had washed to shore and now smelled like the fish trapped in its ropy coils and strap-shaped blades.

She gazed up at the first-quarter moon. She loved the pallid luminescence. She arched her back and slowly opened her arms to receive the moon's light. So much had happened to her. It was still hard to believe. Who she was had remained a mystery to her until she met Maggie Craven, a retired schoolteacher with magic of her own.

"Tu es dea, filia lunae," Maggie told her at their first meeting. "You are a goddess, a Daughter of the Moon." Maggie had explained that in ancient times, when Pandora's box was opened, the last thing to leave the box was hope. Only Selene, the goddess of the moon, saw the demonic creature

lurking nearby that had been sent by the Atrox to devour hope. Selene took pity on humankind and gave her daughters, like guardian angels, to perpetuate hope. Serena was one of those daughters. Then Maggie told her about the Atrox. The Atrox and its Followers had sworn to destroy the Daughters of the Moon because once they were gone, the Atrox could bring about the ruin of humankind.

The words still stunned her. How many people even believed in the mythical world? She had read a few myths in sixth grade, but she didn't think goddesses really existed. And if they did, they wouldn't look like her, funked-out in her great-grandmother's pointy-framed sunglasses, a green stud piercing her nose, a stainless-steel barbell through her tongue, and a hoop through the skin over her belly button. Maggie had laughed and said people judged too much by looks anyway. It was other things that made a goddess, like magnanimity of spirit, courage, and a deep willingness to put one's safety aside to save others. Maggie assured her that Selene had bestowed many gifts on her, but Serena had a bewildering feeling that a darker goddess had also gifted her.

The punkers who had been bothering Morgan today were a new kind of Followers. They weren't like the ones in Hollywood who tried to conceal their identity. These flaunted their allegiance to the Atrox. They were punks with pierced lips, rat's-nest hair, and goat tattoos on their left arms. They used mind control, sucking hope and dreams from their victims. Worse still, they liked blood sports.

She'd ask Maggie about them when she saw her on Thursday. Maggie had become her mentor and guide and Serena loved her like a grandmother or a favored aunt. Before she met Maggie, she had been like a receptor, receiving random thoughts. Sometimes she went days without hearing anything. Other times it felt like there were three radios turned full blast in her head with everyone's thoughts jumbling inside her.

Maggie taught her how to go inside a person's mind. It wasn't easy. The first time she'd tried, she and Maggie had walked over to the

Beverly Center. They sat in the food court at the top of the mall, eating California wraps. Maggie pointed to a young boy and told Serena to concentrate, and in her mind's eye to ease her way into the boy's head.

She did as Maggie had told her and suddenly she was inside the boy's thoughts.

His mind was cluttered. Baseball, soccer, and video games played around her in a dizzy swirl. Then TV shows, movies, and a golden retriever name Harry. Just when she wondered if she was going to be lost forever inside the boy's head, she felt Maggie's hand clasp hers and she was back in the mall, her wrap poised near her mouth.

"Wow" was all she could say.

"That's just the tip of the iceberg." Maggie had smiled. "Wait till you see what you can do."

Even now, when Serena practiced reading a person's mind she would sometimes get caught in their thoughts like a fly in a gluey spider web and panic, thinking she was going to be trapped forever in another person's psyche.

Maggie thought she had mastered her

mind-penetrating skill, not perfectly, but well enough to go on to the next level of power. Now Serena was learning how to take a thought and tuck it deep inside a person's mind so they wouldn't remember it. She called it zapping.

Serena felt a chill and realized she had been wandering aimlessly down the shore for a long time now, enjoying the phosphorescent beauty of the waves. She hurried to a seawall, climbed it, and looked back. She could no longer see the stretch of highway where they had parked the van. She turned to go back when a wave hit the wall and splashed over her. If she went back the way she had come, the incoming tide would cut her off near the rocks. She didn't want to get caught in an unexpected wave, especially in the dark and fog, so she decided she'd better find a way up the bluffs.

By the time she found a path, the fog had pushed into shore, wet and cold. She set down her sandals, untied her sweatshirt, and pulled it over her head. It did little to stop her shivering. Her back ached from the cold and her bare legs were covered with goose bumps. She trudged slowly up the hiking trail through the chaparral. The scrub oaks took on a twisted, haunted look in the darkness.

She walked with care, her uneasiness quickly turning to alarm. She had gone only a little way when she heard a sound as if someone were running in the path ahead of her. The fog was too dense to see.

"Hello!" she yelled.

She cautiously stepped forward.

That's when she heard voices, faint and far away, like a church choir. Singing? No, more like chanting.

She walked quickly now, wanting more than anything to be out of the cold and back in the glare of city lights. Ahead she could see a glow in the fog, and stepped faster. Soon she could make out the cloudy images of people standing around a fire in a clearing ahead. She couldn't imagine anyone having a campfire party on a cold night like this one, but she was grateful she had found them.

Only a few more steps and she could see the fire clearly, with about thirty kids standing in a circle around it. She'd get warm, then ask them the way to the highway. As she walked around the group, no one seemed to notice her. There was a strange tension in the air, as if something important were about to happen.

A girl with long blond hair stood too close to the fire. She wore a low-cut, iridescent black dress; the flowing sleeves reached the tips of her fingers, a gold boa circled her neck, and glittering bracelets curled around her arms. She looked more like she was dressed for a prom than an outdoor party. Flames radiated from the fire and seemed dangerously close to her. Her skirt kept flapping into the blaze.

No one seemed alarmed.

Then the girl smiled, turned, and stepped into the fire.

CHAPTER TWO

N ONE OF THE KIDS standing near the fire seemed concerned. Were they all blasted on forties or high on 'shrooms? Why wasn't anyone doing anything?

Serena dropped her sandals and barreled through the crowd. Her heart raced as adrenaline pumped through her.

The girl's dress billowed, then whipped around her as if she had been caught in a maelstrom. Flames screamed, wrapped around her long hair, and carried it skyward as a log rolled to the edge of the fire with a hiss.

The kids stepped away from the rolling log, but no one made a move to help the girl.

Serena was close enough to the raging flames to hear the crackling logs, but she still couldn't feel the heat. She should have been able to feel its warmth by now.

And then she saw something that made her stop abruptly. Flames seethed around the girl's arms and face in wild delight, but she wasn't burning. She didn't even look like she was suffering. She looked euphoric. Awestruck, Serena stepped closer. It had to be her imagination, but the air seemed colder near the fire.

She hesitated, then brushed her hand through the fire. It flared up. Flames licked the tips of her fingers, and it felt like ice. She pulled her hand back and brushed a thin frost from her skin.

A cold fire? That was impossible. She stared in wonder at the girl in the inferno.

The girl lifted her head to the night sky, spread his arms wide, and smiled.

"*Lecta! Lecta! Lecta!*" the others were chanting. Was that the girl's name?

The flames flickered around the girl's face. She inhaled the fire, then opened her eyes. They shone, phosphorescent. The blaze screeched into the night sky and the girl stepped out.

Serena felt a thrum against her chest. She didn't need to look down to know her amulet was radiating a white light. Its power was like an invisible wave pushing against her in warning. She took an involuntary step backward and quickly looked around. She had stumbled into a gathering of Followers. But why hadn't her amulet warned her earlier? And why weren't they trying to destroy her? They weren't even trying to use their mind control.

That's when she saw Karyl on the other side of the fire. He smiled at her through the sparking flames. Even at this distance she felt something creepy about him, the way he looked at her. The last time she had seen him his mind control had come screeching at her in hellish waves as she faced him in battle. That was the night Karyl, Tymmie, and Cassandra had tried to destroy Catty and Vanessa and steal their powers. She and

Jimena had almost been too late to rescue them, but in the end they had saved the other girls.

She turned and bumped into Tymmie. He was tall, his hair dyed white-blond, the black roots showing. His lips curved in a crooked sort of way. His nose hoops reflected the orange-and-red flames.

"Hey, Goddess." He stepped aside. His thin face still looked haunted but didn't pose a threat.

Cassandra stood on the other side of him, her eyes reflecting the fire. She was wearing stretchy black capris under a black tulle skirt, and silver studded cuffs with a black tank top. Thin white scars on her chest made an S, a T, and an A. She had been madly in love with Stanton, the leader of the Followers, and had tried to slice his name on her chest with a razor blade.

Cassandra looked Serena over. "Cute outfit," she said sarcastically.

Serena glanced at the kids standing around her. They were all dressed as if it were prom night.

Cassandra gave her another venomous glance, then ran her fingers through her maroon-colored hair and stared back at the fire.

Serena backed away, more shaken than if Cassandra had slapped her.

She felt bewildered. She had battled these people once. So why didn't they challenge her now? Was this some kind of trick? A trap?

Then she saw Stanton walking around the fire toward her. He was handsome in a dangerously sexy way in his silky black tuxedo. She knew not to stare into his blue eyes, but there was something compelling that made her eyes linger. Maybe it was the reflection of the fire that made his eyes sparkle with such tenderness. Usually there was a darkness and faraway coldness about them that threatened to drag people into his evil world.

Before she was even aware of it he stood beside her, his eyes inviting and seductive.

"I'm glad you came," he said softly, and stroked her hair sensuously. His eyes held hers. It wasn't terrifying, but comforting and lovely, and that was more frightening than if he had tried to push into her mind and control her.

Her heart began to race painfully in her chest. She staggered backward and stood precariously close to the fire. The smoke billowed around her. She breathed it in. The pungent smell made her dizzy and a little sick to her stomach.

She grabbed her moon amulet and felt an immediate comfort. Maggie had told her that she would always know intuitively what to do, especially when the moon was full. The moon wasn't full, but at least it wasn't a dark moon, which was when she was most vulnerable. Her powers were weakest during those three nights when the moon is invisible from the earth. She tried to clear her mind to think. She felt like running.

A baffled look crossed Stanton's face. "Serena, are you all right?"

"How do you know my name?" she asked as new apprehension filled her. He had never used her name before. He had always called her *Goddess*, the way someone spits out the name of an enemy.

"You told me," he said and circled closer to her. He reached out to touch her again when panic took over and she ran.

"Serena!" he shouted after her.

She crashed through the kids standing near the fire.

Stanton kept calling her name. His footsteps pounded the ground behind her.

It was dangerous to run so near the edge of the bluffs. She ran anyway. Terror shuddered through her and her breath came in rasping draws. Her hands were still quivering, but not from cold now. She was dripping with perspiration. She tried to think. Most of the Followers standing around the fire were probably initiates. Kids who had turned to the Atrox, hoping to be accepted into its congregation. They would want to prove themselves worthy of becoming a Follower. They would have some powers of hypnosis, but her skills were far greater than theirs. They would be no threat, unless a large group of them caught her.

Tymmie, Karyl, and Cassandra had been accepted by the Atrox and were apprenticed to Stanton, learning to perfect their evil. She might be able to fight them off, but Stanton was another matter. He could read minds, manipulate thoughts, and even imprison people in his memories.

She ran more quickly now, arms pumping at her sides. The footsteps behind her were gaining.

That was the last thing she remembered.

Serena awoke with a start on the beach near the seawall. She looked around her, astonished. A moment ago she had been running on the bluffs above the water and the next she was on the beach, lying in the sand. "Stanton?" she called with dread. Her hands were shaking and she felt unbearably cold. When he didn't answer her, she stood slowly, feeling dazed.

She looked in the wet sand. She saw only her own footprints. Could she have fallen asleep and dreamed about the cold fire? She didn't remember resting or even sitting down. She lifted her hand to brush back the hair hanging in her eyes and felt a sharp pain. Her palms were raw and scratched. She stepped down to the water and let a wave wash over them. The salt water stung. Could she have fallen over the bluff, tried to grab hold of something, then slipped and lost consciousness when she hit the sand?

She started walking down the beach. After some distance she heard music coming from Collin's van radio. Relief flowed through her. Never had his irritating, bad-to-the-bone surf guitar music sounded so heavenly.

She turned toward the music and ran up the sand, kicking through discarded cans and the charcoal remains of a long-ago beach fire.

Strong hands grabbed her.

She let out a startled cry.

"Serena?" Collin said in a bewildered voice. His flashlight shone in her eyes, then away. "Where've you been?"

"What do you mean? Why did you stop surfing so early?"

He pushed his waterproof glow-in-the-dark watch in front of her. She stared down at the face of the watch in disbelief. Two hours had passed since the sun had set and she'd left Collin.

"I've been looking for you for almost an hour," he scolded.

She continued to stare at the watch.

"What happened to you?" He took off his jacket and placed it around her shoulders. It was warm from his body heat and she gratefully snuggled into it.

"You're shivering and—"

"And what?" She tried to push into his mind to see what he was seeing but her own mind felt sluggish.

"How'd you break your glasses?"

She took them off the top of her head. The lens was missing from the right side.

"I don't know." She hated the tremble of fear that had crept into her words.

"What do you mean *you don't know?*"

She shrugged.

"Did you fall on the rocks?"

She shook her head, even though she knew he couldn't see her in the dark.

"You didn't try to climb up the cliff, did you?" he asked.

"Maybe." She tried to force herself to remember. "I must have fallen."

"You know how dangerous that is!" He sounded really upset.

They walked back toward the van in silence, following the bobbing beam of his flashlight. Soon streetlights from the highway cast a dim light over the beach.

Finally she was able to steady herself enough to speak without the strange twitch in her words. "I don't know what happened," she said. "I thought I was on top of the bluffs, but then I woke up in the sand like I had fallen asleep."

He opened the van door and the dome light came on. She glanced up and saw the worry on Collin's face. She wondered what he was seeing on her own face, because he held her hands tightly.

"Are you sure you're all right?" And in the same breath he said, "You're lucky paramedics aren't scraping you off the rocks."

He opened her hands and looked at the palms. They were scratched, as if she had fallen and tried to grab hold of something.

She closed her hands into fists.

"Let's get out of here," she said and slipped into the passenger side of the utility van. She pressed her bare feet into the carpet. What had happened to her blue sandals? She touched the top of her head and squinted, trying to remember. It only made her feel dizzy. The fire seemed hazy now, like a dream. The more she tried to pull it into focus, the more it drifted away.

"Serena."

She became aware then that Collin had been talking to her.

"Do you want to go to the hospital?"

"No," she said.

"Sure?"

"Yeah."

She felt his hand touch her head and then she looked at the tips of his fingers. A single drop of blood sat on the top of his index finger.

"You must have hit your head," he said. "Maybe we should go to the hospital."

"I'm fine." She tried to sound convincing as she pulled down the mirror on the visor. She examined the small scrape. "It's not deep."

"Promise me that you'll stay away from the bluffs," he said.

"I promise." But she didn't think she had fallen. She would remember slipping, trying to hold on, the freefall.

"Home?" he asked. The concern in his eyes made her feel guilty.

"Yeah, turn on the heat," she said and pulled the seat belt around her. She hated the unclear feeling inside her head. She clasped her arms around her for warmth. Even the familiar smells of surf wax, zinc oxide, and suntan oil didn't comfort her the way they normally would. She wanted to be away from this beach that had once been such a place of solace.

Collin jumped behind the wheel and turned on the engine, then the heater.

She turned and looked toward the cliffs, hoping to see the faint glow from a fire through the fog. She didn't see anything. Maybe Collin was right. Maybe she had fallen.

He pulled into the fog-locked traffic and turned the music higher.

By the time they merged onto the Santa Monica Freeway, her heart rhythm had returned to normal.

"How was it?" she asked finally.

"The skeg was humming," he said. A skeg was the tail of the surfboard and humming was the whistle the skeg made cutting at high speed through the water.

Her mind felt less fuzzy now and she gently pushed into Collin's mind to see if he had seen anything that might give her a clue about what had happened. She didn't find anything unusual, but twice he glanced at her as if he could feel her sorting through his thoughts. What would he do if he found out she could read his mind?

CHAPTER THREE

*S*ATURDAY MORNING, the aroma of baking muffins filled Serena's warm kitchen. Her pet raccoon, Wally, paced near his food dish, his nails clicking impatiently on the floor. Serena sipped her now cold coffee and finished telling Jimena about the night before.

"And then I woke up on the beach by the seawall," she finished.

"That's it?" Jimena asked.

"It."

Jimena leaned against the cupboard, deep in thought, and raked her hands through her long black hair. Her hooded, zip-front sweater hid the tattoos on her arms, remnants from her days in a gang, but the tattoo on her belly peeked over the top of her hip-huggers.

"That's some bad stuff." Jimena shook her head. "Feed Wally while I think."

Serena filled a bowl with grapes, then mixed a can of cat food with some baby food on another plate.

Jimena helped her set the food on the floor, then she sat on the counter and swung her long legs in and out of the sunlight cascading through the windows. "It had to be a dream," she decided, and counted on her fingers. Her nails were long and painted turquoise. "First, I would have had a premonition, *sin duda*, if you were going to meet up with a group of Followers."

"Probably," Serena agreed.

That was Jimena's gift. She had premonitions about the future. She was almost always forewarned if one of them was going to have a serious run-in with the Followers. It was creepy to think that she could see the future, especially because she had never been able to stop any of her premonitions from coming true, no matter how bad they were.

"Second, no one can stay in a fire that long and survive. If the Followers could, Maggie would have told us."

Maggie had introduced Jimena and Serena a year back. At first it had been a very reluctant friendship. Jimena had been deep in a gang, jacking cars and hanging out with her home girls. No way was she going to be friends with a wimp like Serena. Serena had liked that Jimena never played games the way most girls did, saying one thing and doing another. That made it easy for Serena to respect her. The first time they had fought a group of Followers, Jimena had changed her mind about Serena. Serena had never backed down. Now Jimena trusted Serena with her life.

"Third," she said as Serena pulled the muffins from the oven, "the fire felt cold. That's dream stuff."

Serena took the muffins from the tin and set them in a basket.

"What's fourth?" Serena had caught Jimena's thought. She carried the muffins to the table and set them next to the butter and a carafe of coffee.

Jimena jumped off the counter and followed her. She sat down and buttered a muffin. Steam curled into the air as the butter melted. "Fourth, you wouldn't be here if you'd met up with a gang of Followers."

Serena nodded, but the explanation didn't feel right. She knew there was more, but she couldn't seem to work her mind around it. She slumped back in her chair. "Stanton chased me."

"You told me."

"I think he caught me." Serena slipped Collin's cozy sweater off her shoulder. She showed Jimena the bruises on her arm that looked as if someone had grabbed her hard.

Jimena touched the four round bruises near her shoulder.

"You must have done it yourself on the rocks," Jimena assured her. "You'd remember if someone grabbed you."

"Maybe," Serena said. "Remember last month when the Followers caught Morgan and stole her hope?"

Jimena nodded.

"She was all dazed," Serena continued. "And didn't know what had happened to her. Maybe that's what happened to me."

"Followers don't want *your* hope. They want you, *Serenita.*"

"Still . . ."

"Don't worry about it," Jimena assured her. "Worry can't do nothing to protect you. Friends are for that, and I got your back."

"Thanks." Serena chewed the side of her mouth, thinking. "It's just weird not to be able to remember what happened for almost two hours. Maybe I should tell Maggie."

Jimena gave her a curious look. "You'll have to wait until Thursday, when we meet her for tea. She won't be back until then, remember?"

Serena started to answer when the back door opened and Collin walked in.

"Hey," he greeted them. He wore vans,

low-slung baggies, and a bad mood. He'd just come back from an early morning at the beach and hadn't bothered to wipe the zinc oxide off his nose and bottom lip.

"How was it?" Serena asked.

"Waves were awesome." Collin opened the refrigerator and pulled out a quart of milk. He stood in the open refrigerator, swallowed the milk, then tossed the carton in the trash and slammed the refrigerator.

From the scrape marks on the side of his leg, Serena figured he'd wiped out. He must have hurt himself to quit so early.

Suddenly, his nose drained. He tried to catch the water with the back of his hand, then grabbed a dish towel and wiped his chin and nose.

"*Tienes mocos,*" Jimena laughed. "You are such a faucet nose."

Collin frowned. After a grueling surf session his nasal passages filled with sea water, and then drained at embarrassing times.

"I thought you never wiped out?" Jimena

added with a big grin. "Didn't you tell me a faucet nose was caused by having water forced up your nose during a wipeout?"

"Look, *ghetto*," Collin said with a burst of anger that wasn't like him. "You don't even know what a wipeout is." He started rummaging noisily through the cupboards.

"*Oye, mocoso.*" Jimena stood, her chair scraped back. "Who you calling *ghetto*?"

"You." Collin slammed a cupboard door.

Jimena took her attitude stance and now the air prickled with rising tension.

"Over in El Monte, they call you the kook of Malibu." Jimena danced with her words, spreading the syllables long with a superexaggerated Mexican accent that normally she didn't have.

Serena shook her head. "Kook" was an especially derogatory term, meaning someone who lived inland and got in the way of real surfers by doing something impossibly stupid like abandoning a surfboard so that it caused a major wipeout for someone else.

Collin's eyes lingered on Jimena. "Yeah, well,

it was a fool kook who caused me to wipe out today, probably one of your ghetto friends."

"Please." Serena rolled her eyes. "Do you guys have to fight every time you see each other?"

Collin grabbed a muffin, eyes still focused on Jimena, and shoved it in his mouth as if he were purposely trying to gross her out by eating with his mouth open.

She shook her head. "I've seen blood and brains, little boy, you think you're going to gross me out with bad table manners?" Jimena cleared her throat as if startled by a memory that had been conjured up. She turned to Serena. "So what you looking for in the garage sales today?"

Collin tapped the edge of the table angrily. "Later," he said, and trundled out of the kitchen.

"Fringed poncho, maybe." Serena watched Collin leave the room.

"I want some of those psychedelic polyester shirts." Jimena sipped her coffee.

"We better go." Serena stood. She wished her brother and her best friend wouldn't fight so much.

They left the house and started walking over to Fairfax Avenue. They walked in silence for a while, then Serena spoke. "Can you believe what Morgan said about me needing a boyfriend?"

"That's her life." Jimena shrugged. "She can't live without a guy."

"It's not like it's exactly easy for us to have boyfriends," Serena said.

"Yeah," Jimena agreed. "Every time I meet some *reteguapo* guy, the more I like him, the more premonitions I get about him. The more premonitions I get about him, the more I don't like him. It takes the magic out when I see him sneaking around and doing things he doesn't even know he's going to do yet. Only Veto was true to me, but then he ends up dead." Her words turned hoarse.

"Well, at least none of them are calling you weird," Serena offered.

Jimena laughed so loudly that the people lined up to eat at Red turned and looked at her. "I wish I could have seen you sitting there, all pretty and *suavecita*, saying 'thank you' and 'I like you, too,' when he hadn't even said a word to you."

"But I never got mad at a guy for something he hadn't even done yet," Serena shot back.

"Yeah," Jimena considered. "Who wants a boyfriend anyway? Guys are a mess of hormones and sweat."

"Me?" Serena said weakly.

Jimena smiled at her. "*Yo tambien*, but different this time. I don't want to know all about the future with him. I don't want to see his death coming, or see him messing with some *ruca*. Someone like your brother. That's what I want."

Serena stopped suddenly, and two Hassidic men on their way to temple almost bumped into her. "You hate my brother!"

"I mean some *vato* like your brother but *not* your brother," Jimena corrected.

"What do you mean?"

"*Con tu hermano*, the only thing I ever see him doing in the future is riding a wave."

They were silent for a long time, then Serena spoke hesitantly, "You ever think that maybe we're not supposed to have boyfriends because of what happens when we turn seventeen?"

"I had Veto," Jimena whispered.

"And he died," Serena finished for her.

Jimena nodded. "Maybe we're not."

Their gifts only lasted until they were seventeen. Then, Maggie had explained, there was a metamorphosis. They had to make the most important choice of their lives. Either they could lose their powers and the memory of what they had once been, or they disappeared. The ones who disappeared became something else, guardian spirits perhaps. No one really knew. They didn't talk about it much. It was too frightening.

"Vanessa has a boyfriend," Serena added hopefully.

"Yeah, but she almost didn't," Jimena pointed out.

Vanessa had the power to become invisible, but when she became really emotional, her molecules began to separate on their own. When Vanessa had first started dating Michael Saratoga her molecules had gone out of control, and she had started to go invisible every time he tried to kiss her.

"There they are." Serena pointed down the street.

Catty and Vanessa were vamping it up on the corner of Fairfax and Beverly, in bell-bottoms with exaggerated lacy bells that they must have pulled from Catty's mother's closet.

Vanessa gave them the peace sign. "Feelin' groovy." She winked. She had gorgeous skin, movie-star blue eyes, and flawless blond hair. She was wearing a headband and blue-tinted glasses. Catty was forever getting Vanessa into trouble, but they remained best friends.

"Love and peace," Catty greeted them. Catty was stylish in an artsy sort of way. Right now, she wore a hand-knit cap with pom-pom ties that hung down to her waist, and her puddle-jumping Doc Martens were so wrong with the bell-bottoms that they looked totally right. Her curly brown hair poked from beneath the fuchsia cap and her brown eyes were framed by granny glasses, probably another steal from her mother.

"You like our retro look?" Vanessa giggled at all the cars honking at them.

"Yeah, but what's that smell?" Jimena sniffed.

"Mom's aromatherapy." Catty rolled her eyes. "It's lavender, so I won't be so stressed out."

"When were you ever stressed out?" Serena hooted.

"Never," Catty answered "Mom just thinks everyone is stressed."

Serena smiled. "It doesn't smell so bad."

"I don't think I'll be borrowing it." Jimena wrinkled her nose.

Maggie had brought them all together and was still showing them how to use their special powers to fight the Atrox and its Followers. According to Maggie, they were an unstoppable force, but that's not how they felt. More often they felt as if their powers controlled them.

Vanessa waved a newspaper. She had circled and numbered the garage sales and brought a map.

"The first sale is only a block away." She started in the direction of Fairfax Avenue.

Serena told them about the cold fire and the girl named Lecta as they walked down a side street.

"It had to be a dream," Vanessa said. "The fire was cold."

"If they were acting like they wanted to party, maybe you did some act of kindness to them so they couldn't hurt you," Catty said.

"I'm sure I didn't," Serena said. A Follower could never harm a person who had done a genuine act of kindness toward him or her. Serena looked at Vanessa. Once Stanton had trapped Vanessa in his childhood memories. While she was there she had tried to save a younger Stanton from the Atrox. For that he could never harm her.

"Do you know anyone named Lecta?" Vanessa asked.

"No," Serena admitted.

"It was a dream," Catty insisted. "The girl didn't burn."

"That's what I've been telling her," Jimena agreed.

"Yeah." Serena scowled. "But it felt so real."

"Haven't you ever had one of those dreams where you want to wake up but you can't, then when you finally do, you feel relieved what happened was only a dream?"

"Sure." Serena nodded. "But this was different."

"There's one way to find out," Catty cut in as they reached the first garage sale.

Serena picked up a jeweled necklace with a small drop pearl surrounded by garnets. "Which is?" She held the necklace across her forehead.

"Looks hot." Jimena admired it.

"Yeah, it's looks like a headache band like they wore in the twenties." Vanessa examined it.

"Excuse me," Catty interrupted. "But I had a terrific idea."

"What?" Serena pulled a dollar from her pocket to pay the lady holding the sale. She slipped the necklace into her pocket.

"It's easy." Catty smiled. "I'll go back in time and check it out."

Catty had the freakiest power. She could actually go back and forth in time. She missed a lot of school because she was always twisting time. But her mother didn't care, because she knew Catty was different. She wasn't Catty's biological mother. She'd found Catty walking along the side of the road in the Arizona desert when Catty was six years old. She was going to turn her over to the authorities in Yuma, but when she saw Catty make time change, she decided Catty was an extraterrestrial, and that it was her duty to protect her from government officials who would probably dissect her. She still didn't know that Catty was a goddess. Somehow it was easier for people to believe in space aliens than in goddesses.

"So who wants to go with me?"

"No, thanks." Vanessa shuddered. "I hate the tunnel." The tunnel was what she called the hole in time that Catty had to travel through to get from one time to the next. Besides Catty, Vanessa was the only one who had been in it.

"How 'bout you?" Catty elbowed Serena. "You're always bugging me to take you back."

Serena shook her head. "Not this trip." She had wanted to try it out even after hearing Vanessa describe the dank, burnt-cabbage smell of the tunnel and thrill-ride feel of the travel. She wasn't even afraid of the landings. Vanessa had told her that when they arrived at their destination, they fell back into time, which felt like falling on granite. Plus Catty was seldom accurate in her landings. They might land miles away, and near the ocean that could mean really bad news. Still, Serena would have been willing to risk it, if the memories of last night with the Followers hadn't been haunting her.

"I don't want to run into the Followers," Serena said simply. "Go someplace else and I'll go with you."

"*Please,* your landings are way off, and you'd have to land next to the bluffs and the ocean," Vanessa cautioned.

"Jeez, I've been practicing so much and you guys still don't trust me," Catty complained, and twirled the pom-poms on her cap, then looked slyly at Jimena. "You sure you don't want to go?" Catty's eyes began to dilate as if power were surging in her brain, and she reached out for Jimena's hand.

"Look, the trip only takes minutes for you," Serena said. "But the rest of us have to relive the whole night, and I know that's something I don't want to do." But it was too late. She could already feel the change around her, as if the air pressure were dropping. She glanced at Catty's watch. The hands started to move backward.

"Stop!" Vanessa yelled. Her hair stood out with a charge of static electricity.

When Catty didn't stop, Jimena grabbed Serena and Vanessa. "Hold your amulets."

They each grasped the moon amulet hanging around their necks.

"Meet you at Kokomo's," Jimena yelled before Catty disappeared in a blinding flash of white light. The air settled.

"Why didn't we go back?" Vanessa looked around, baffled.

"Maggie told me holding the amulet is a way for us to stay in the present when Catty travels back in time," Jimena explained. "I was supposed to tell you. Sorry. Forgot."

"Why did you see Maggie?" Serena asked.

"Premonition," Jimena answered. "I saw her just before she left."

It wasn't unusual for Jimena to have a premonition that she needed to discuss with Maggie, but this time Serena had an uneasy feeling that there was something more she wasn't telling. But she let her suspicion slip away. Jimena had never kept anything from her before.

Vanessa was thoughtful for a moment, then she spoke. "Catty says all time exists at once. We just experience it one day at a time because that's the way we've been taught to think about it. I guess she's right. We're here. She's there. Kind of freaky."

"It's freaky, all right." Serena thought of Catty back at the cold beach while they were safe in the warm sunshine. She wondered what Catty was seeing.

At the fourth garage sale, Vanessa's stomach growled. "I'm hungry, and Catty should be getting back by now."

Serena, Vanessa, and Jimena walked down Fairfax toward Farmers Market. Buses brought tourists to the open-air market for souvenir shopping and dining. There were so many places to eat that it was almost impossible to choose.

They found a table under an umbrella at Kokomo's and sat down.

A constant procession of tourists wove in and out of the tables at the small open-air restaurant and gawked at the glossy autographed photos of celebrities on the wall over the counter. The tourists peered at the girls, hoping to recognize someone famous. Vanessa, Jimena, and Catty were used to it because they had grown up in Los Angeles. Serena had come from Long Beach, and tourists on the *Queen Mary* weren't looking for movie stars.

Vanessa looked at her watch as the waiter came to their table. "Catty's taking too long," she whispered.

"We shouldn't have let her go," Jimena said.

"You girls decided yet?" the waiter asked impatiently.

"Give us a few more minutes," Vanessa answered.

The waiter went to the next table.

Suddenly strange currents shimmered like heat waves in the air and a change in air pressure made people look at the sky as if they expected to see a storm brewing. Serena could feel the hair on the back of her neck rise.

Catty fell in a heap on the blacktop walkway next to their table.

People around them turned and stared.

"Where'd she come from?" a woman with thick dark glasses asked.

"Must have fallen off the roof," a man commented.

The waiter looked at Catty as if he'd found a cockroach on the table.

"Hi." Catty stood. She was soaking wet. A long strand of kelp wrapped around her arm. Without missing a beat, she turned and faced the gathering crowd. "Don't forget to see *Ocean Deep*, coming soon to your local theater."

Tourists clicked pictures, and some applauded.

"Hollywood." Catty laughed even though she was shivering.

Vanessa, Jimena, and Serena gathered around her.

"What happened to you?" Vanessa pulled the kelp off Catty's arm.

"Yeah." Serena took off Collin's sweater and placed it around Catty.

"More important," Jimena said, "what did you see?"

"My landing was way screwed up," Catty explained. "I landed in the ocean and had to swim for shore."

"Why didn't you just come back right away?" Vanessa asked.

"I couldn't." Catty shrugged. "I panicked."

Serena pushed into Catty's mind. She saw the dark and felt the cold water draining Catty's strength as she swam toward the sound of the surf.

Vanessa hugged Catty. "You've got to be more careful."

Serena shivered and came back from the place in Catty's mind. "Let's go to my house," she suggested. "It's closest."

"Maybe we should go to my house," Vanessa said, too quickly.

"You always do that," Serena turned to face her. "Whenever Catty's with us you never want to go to my house. What's up?"

"That's not true," Vanessa said defensively.

"Yeah, it is," Jimena piped up.

"True," Catty added. "What's at Serena's house you don't want me to see?"

"Don't be silly." Vanessa waved them away. "You're just imagining it."

Catty and Serena looked at each other and nodded.

Serena crept inside Vanessa's mind and tried to find the reason Vanessa didn't want Catty to go over to Serena's house. She pushed around memories of Michael, peeked at the homework—she had no idea Vanessa studied so much—and then she found the memories of Vanessa's visits to her home, but she didn't find anything to give her a clue. She slipped back out.

Vanessa was staring at her. "That's creepy, Serena."

"What gave it away?" Serena asked.

"I was suddenly thinking about all my homework!" Vanessa laughed. "You must have accidentally pushed the memories to the front of my brain."

Serena shrugged. They turned down Beverly and soon they were in Serena's warm kitchen. Serena gave Catty a pair of clean sweats.

"You can change in the downstairs bathroom, it's right next to the washer and dryer. There's a shower, too, if you want."

"Thanks." Catty disappeared into the utility room next to the kitchen.

"She's lucky she didn't drown." Vanessa shook her head and took cocoa from a cupboard.

"We shouldn't have let her go." Serena placed a pan on top of the stove as Jimena pulled milk from the refrigerator.

That's when they heard Catty scream. They ran to the utility porch.

Catty bumped into them. "There's a wild animal in your bathroom!"

Serena pushed past her and ran into the

bathroom. Wally leaned into the toilet, meticulously cleaning a grape.

"That's just Wally." Serena lifted her pet raccoon from the toilet. She wiped his paws with a towel and carried him back to Catty. "I should have warned you, but I just thought Vanessa would have told you."

Vanessa got a strange look on her face. "Oops."

"That's it?" Serena asked. "You didn't want Catty to know about Wally? Why not?"

Before Vanessa could answer, Catty spoke. "I can't believe you took a wild animal out of its natural habitat and keep it as a pet. It's drinking out of the toilet!"

"He would have died if I hadn't taken him. His mom abandoned him. And he wasn't drinking out of the toilet," Serena corrected. "He was washing a grape."

Catty shook her head. "They have shelters for wild animals who are deserted." She turned to Vanessa. "I can't believe you didn't tell me. We've got to do something."

Vanessa rolled her eyes. "See?"

"So what are you going to do about it?" Jimena joked. "Turn Serena in?" She took Wally from Serena and handed him to Catty. The raccoon licked her ear, then started grooming her wet hair.

Catty petted Wally. "Well, he doesn't seem like he's suffering. I guess living with Serena is better than being dead."

"Thanks," Serena said sarcastically.

"Sorry." Catty smiled. "I didn't mean—"

Then Catty looked really serious. "Just don't anyone tell my mother. Ever!" She put Wally down and went back to the bathroom to shower and change her clothes.

A few minutes later Catty joined them, smelling of soap. They sat around the kitchen table drinking hot cocoa and Catty told them everything that had happened. "Once I swam to shore I hiked up the cliff near the seawall, but I didn't see anything. No fire. Not even a smoky smell."

"Then I must have fallen." Serena focused on

her memories of that night. "But it felt so real."

"We better tell Maggie anyway." Jimena looked around the group.

"When we have tea with her on Thursday," Vanessa added.

"Okay," Serena agreed, and tossed another marshmallow into her cocoa.

Catty picked up the deck of tarot cards that were sitting on the table and placed them in front of Serena. "Read our fortune. Do it for all of us at once." There was too much excitement in her voice, as if she were trying to lift the solemn mood that had settled over Serena.

"I don't know if it can work that way," Serena said.

"Try," Catty coaxed.

Serena shuffled the cards. "I'll just do a three-card spread. Everyone think of their question while I shuffle." She glanced up. They were all staring at her. She didn't need to read their minds to know they were all asking about the cold fire. "Okay, so now each of you divide the deck so that we have three stacks that are facedown. One for past, one for the near future, and one for the final outcome."

Each of them divided the cards, then Serena turned over the first card from the first stack. "The devil." She frowned. "Not a good sign."

"What does it mean?" Catty asked.

"It means that we've entered a negative cycle and our problems are going to multiply. We won't be able to see the whole picture clearly."

"Too weird." Catty was hushed.

"Go on." Vanessa nodded.

Serena snapped the card from the second stack and placed it on the table.

"The moon." Jimena smiled. "That's got to be a good sign for us."

"No," Serena whispered. "This card represents what is about to be. Things are not going to go smoothly because of some deception."

"Yikes." Catty's eyes widened.

"They're just cards," Vanessa reassured them. "They don't mean anything, really. Turn over the next one."

Serena did. "The high priestess." Her hand

started shaking and she quickly dropped the card and hid her hand under the table.

They all stared at her.

"Well?" Catty demanded. "What's the outcome?"

Serena scooped up the cards. "Let's try again."

She shuffled, then let them divide the stack. She took the first card, then the second and the third. The devil, the moon, and the high priestess came up again in the same order.

"Quit fooling around," Jimena scolded.

Serena sighed. "I'm not."

"What does the high priestess mean?" Vanessa wondered.

Serena tapped her finger on the card. "We're at a crossroads and the outcome will be different from what we expect."

"That doesn't have to mean anything bad," Vanessa said hopefully.

Serena cleared her throat. "Changes are taking place." She didn't like the way the high priestess card seemed to be warning her.

"Forget it." Catty stood up. "Cards can't tell the future anyway. Besides, I'm bored with cards. Let's practice dancing."

"That's a good idea." Jimena turned on the radio. "*Hay que ser muy desinhibida para esto,* Vanessa."

"What's she telling me?" Vanessa moved her feet with the beat of the music.

"You got to be uninhibited," Catty teased.

"How'd you know?" Vanessa asked. "You don't speak Spanish."

"'Cause you always freeze up! And if you want to impress Michael you're going to have to let your butt swing!"

Vanessa took a deep breath and followed Jimena's lead.

"*Con más sensualidad.*" Jimena swayed her hips.

"I understood that one." Vanessa smiled.

Serena was still staring at the cards.

"Come on." Jimena took her hand and pulled her away from the table.

Serena fell in line behind Jimena but kept glancing back at the devil card. The creature drawn on the face of the card had the head and feet of a he-goat and the bosom and arms of a woman. "It's the tarot's mystery card," she whispered. "It's never good."

"Stop," Vanessa admonished. "We need to practice our new dance steps so our crew will look hot when Michael's band plays at Planet Bang."

"So *you'll* look hot," Catty corrected.

"Yup!" Vanessa answered with delight.

"All right." Serena tried to concentrate on dancing, but the cards kept drawing her eyes back, as if to warn her of something important.

MONDAY AT SCHOOL Serena set her cello down and opened her locker slowly. Chopin's Sonata in G Minor was still on her mind. She would need to increase her practice time if she was going to be able to play the sonata perfectly for the winter concert. She could mark the measures with which she was having the most difficulty and begin with those, exercising her fingers until they ran smoothly over the fast runs.

She held the locker door open, pulled out her algebra book, and slipped her music back inside.

◄ 7 0 ►

Someone nudged the locker door shut.

She turned sharply and took in a quick gulp of air.

Zahi leaned against the row of lockers. He had moved to California from France two weeks ago. His black hair fell in his eyes and he casually brushed it back. A gold stud glistened in his left ear. She loved his angular face, his clear brown eyes, his French accent and European charm.

"And how are you today, Serena?" He had the most wonderful accent she had ever heard.

She wished she could control the blush rising to her cheeks. "Hi." She tossed him an insolent smile. She might as well wear a neon sign: *Serena Killingsworth has a major crush on Zahi, new boy at school, incredible looker who is also smart and speaks French and—*

"I heard that you can read my future in your tarot cards." He looked at her with open interest.

"Who told you that?" she teased.

"Morgan told me."

"Morgan, huh?" Serena tilted her head. They had been talking to each other a little more each day and she was sure that he liked her at least half as much as she liked him. Did he want her to read the cards so he would have an excuse to visit her? She glanced at his eyes. She couldn't pull away. The only other guy this good-looking at school was Michael Saratoga, and he was totally devoted to Vanessa.

"If you can see the future, should I be scared of you?" He rested his hand on the top of the lockers so that his arm was close enough for her to feel the heat radiating from his body.

"Maybe." She leaned toward him, daring him to put his arm around her. She loved the way he looked at her. "You don't have to be afraid of me." She spoke the words like an invitation. "It's just for fun. I'll read your spread for free." Did that seem too desperate? Guys usually couldn't get to her like this. What was it about him that made her feel so strangely wonderful?

"I'll read coffee for you."

"You mean tea?" she asked.

"No. Where I come from, the coffee is so strong that you turn the cup over when you are finished drinking it and read the dregs."

"I didn't know they did that in France."

"I speak French," he explained, "and my family lived in France, but we come from Morocco. I also speak Arabic." He whispered the last word and it brushed lazily across her cheek.

She picked up her cello and started walking.

He walked with her. "Do you find me at all interesting?"

"What?" She stopped and looked at him.

"Or maybe you belong to a very serious religious group? One perhaps that does not allow you to talk to the boys?"

"Why would you think that?"

"All this week I've been trying to get you to invite me to your house and so far I have had no luck." He let his hand run down her arm. She felt herself drifting at the sight of his lazy smile. She didn't move her arm.

"Well?" He stretched slowly, lifting his books over his head. His black turtleneck pulled up and she caught a glimpse of a sun tattooed around his belly button.

"Sure, you can come over." She cleared her throat and looked down at her fuchsia cashmere tube top and feather-trimmed zebra-print slacks, then smiled flirtatiously. "Would someone into a way serious religion dress the way I do?"

He laughed. The sound was full and rich and made her want to hug him. "That is why I wanted to meet you. You dress like a Christmas tree. I'm an artist. I love color and style. Look down the hallway—you would think they were winter birds, would you not? All black and gray and navy blue. You are from a tropical paradise."

She hadn't thought of it before. The sun was shining but the hallways looked dark. Then she glanced at him. He was wearing a tight black turtleneck, black jeans, black boots, and a thick black belt with a curious silver buckle.

"You should talk!" She laughed.

"I like the way you laugh." He pressed closer to her.

She pushed into his mind for one quick glimpse. She concentrated and was immediately filled with joy. His memories and thoughts were all in French and Arabic. Maybe she could finally have a real boyfriend. No way could she answer this guy's thoughts. She couldn't understand a word.

"Of what are you thinking now?" A slow easy smile crossed his face.

"I don't speak a word of French," she said. "Or Arabic."

"That makes you so happy?"

"Maybe." She tilted her head. "We'll see."

"Do you always smile so much?" he asked. "It is as if you have a big secret."

If he only knew her secrets.

"Yeah, I guess I have a couple secrets," she teased.

"Tell them to me," he whispered.

"Can't." She shook her head.

"I like your tongue pierce." He touched her bottom lip.

Her heart flipped. The way he was looking at her, the light touch of his finger on her lip . . .

His face suddenly turned serious and he

leaned forward. "I like you, Serena." His hands caressed her cheeks.

She wanted to kiss him, right there in the middle of the hallway with kids pushing all around them.

He fixed his eyes on her as if he could read her thoughts and he grabbed her free hand. "I want my invitation first."

"Zahi." She tried to say his name as if she hadn't practiced it in front of her mirror at home. "Why don't you come over to my house tonight?"

He leaned closer and she wondered if he was going to kiss her. Then she heard a commotion down the hallway, and the moment was gone.

They broke apart and turned. Morgan was walking toward them. She wore a leather maxi coat over a slinky short red dress, and black suede boots that came above her knees. Her hair was all sunlight and shimmer. Every guy turned his head and made a comment or gave a whistle as she passed.

Zahi stared at Morgan. He probably had a major crush on her, like most of the guys at school.

"Ah, Morgan," Serena commented dryly.

"You are prettier." He playfully touched her chin.

"I'm afraid that's not so."

"Yes, so," he insisted with a melting smile. "You have class and style that show you think for yourself. Morgan is a page from a fashion magazine." He touched her arm lightly. "I have to go on to my next class now. The teacher hates late arrivers. I will see you soon, no?" He ran backward, watching her, before he finally turned and sprinted away.

"Class and style," she whispered after him.

Jimena, Vanessa, and Catty came up behind her. "Why are you looking so dreamy?" Jimena studied her.

"Zahi," Catty answered with a sly smile. "It's only completely obvious she likes him."

"He's really cute." Vanessa looked him over appreciatively.

"Serena likes 'em brooding and tortured," Jimena added.

"He's artistic," Serena defended.

"How are you going to kiss him with that barbell through your tongue?" Jimena asked, pushing her playfully.

"Kiss him?" Serena hadn't really thought about the barbell getting in the way. Would it? She had never gotten to kiss her last boyfriend, and the only other kisses she had had were the awkward pecks from games of spin the bottle in sixth grade, long before she had ever pierced her tongue.

"Isn't that what couples do?" Vanessa smiled in a pensive kind of way.

"Unless they go invisible," Catty teased.

"That's not funny." Vanessa was still sensitive about the difficulty she'd had kissing Michael. Probably because she was afraid it could happen again.

"Just don't lick his face like they do in the movies," Jimena said. "Guys hate that."

"How do you know?" Catty joked. "Have you licked someone's face?"

"Listen to the voice of experience," Jimena bragged. "Don't lean in too fast—you'll chip your teeth. And if he shoves his tongue down your throat—"

"Gross!" Vanessa, Catty, and Serena said in unison.

"This is real life, *chicas*." Jimena crossed her arms. "You want to hear or not?"

Serena raised her hand. "Yeah, I want to hear."

"Me, too," Vanessa chimed in.

"If he jams his tongue in your mouth, pull away and smile at him. He'll figure it out if you keep doing that."

"What if he doesn't?"

"Then you stick the tip of your tongue into his mouth so he can see that a kiss is not supposed to require a Heimlich maneuver."

"You guys are pathetic," a voice said snidely.

They turned and Morgan was standing by her locker. "If you like someone it comes naturally."

"Maybe you always kiss guys who have done a lot of smooching." Catty grinned wickedly. "The rest of us date guys who aren't disease-ridden."

"That's *so* not funny," Morgan said. "Besides, when have you ever had a date, Catty?"

"*No seas pesada,*" Jimena muttered in a low voice.

"What?" Morgan twisted her head around.

"She said don't be a pain in the butt, Morgan." Catty arched her brows. "You going to do something about it?"

Morgan glanced at Jimena.

Jimena held her head back and glared at her.

"Who's planning on getting kissed, anyway?" Morgan pulled a strawberry gloss from her locker and rubbed it on her lips.

No one answered her.

"It's not like I'm not going to find out," she said and eyed Jimena as if she were the enemy.

Jimena cocked her head and folded her arms over her chest.

Catty rolled her eyes. "Since when is it your business, anyway?"

Morgan pulled her books from her locker. "As if I really care." She looked at them derisively. "You going to be home this afternoon, Serena?"

"Yeah, maybe, why?"

"No reason." Morgan slammed her locker closed and slunk back down the hallway.

"Man, that girl gets on my nerves." Serena watched Morgan stroll away from them.

Vanessa spoke up. "You guys should give her a chance."

They all turned and looked at Vanessa in disbelief.

"She only, like, tried to steal Michael from you," Serena pointed out.

"And I bet she still would," Catty added.

The bell rang and they all ran for class.

Serena quickly forgot about Morgan and started planning for Zahi's visit. She wondered if she should bake chocolate chip cookies. She decided to stop on the way home and buy some chocolate chips at Ralph's.

Serena stared out the kitchen window. The smells of freshly baked cookies wafted through the kitchen. A pale gibbous moon hung in the sky, even though the sun hadn't set yet.

"These cookies are your best ever," Jimena said behind her and spread her khaki pants on the table. "We should start selling them. Seriously."

The back door opened and Collin walked in.

"Hey," he said. His nose and lips were still covered with white zinc oxide.

"*Oye*, Serena, a *payaso* just walked into your kitchen!"

"Don't you ever go home?" Collin looked annoyed. He scooped up a handful of cookies.

"Those cookies aren't for you," Jimena informed him. "They're for Zahi."

"Zahi?" Collin asked. "Who's that?"

Serena felt herself panic. Now Collin would know a boy was coming over. Would he play guardian as usual?

"Zahi is a friend of Serena's," Jimena explained.

Collin looked at Serena. "Have I ever met this guy?"

"No." Serena kept her voice light. "He just moved here."

Collin sat down at the table. "Maybe I'd better meet him, then."

"Don't you have a life of your own?" Jimena mocked. "If you got a girlfriend, you wouldn't need to play chaperone to Serena."

Collin glared at her. "Yeah, I need a pain in the butt like you."

Jimena's eyes sparked with fire.

"Would you guys *stop*?" Serena couldn't take it anymore.

Collin glanced at the clock. "Later," he blurted and left the kitchen.

"He's such a little——" Jimena started.

Serena interrupted her. "Do you ever think that the reason the two of you clash all the time is because you secretly like each other?"

"*Mira*, Serena." Jimena laughed. "You can read my mind, so you know that's not the truth."

The doorbell rang.

Serena ran to answer it, hoping to find Zahi. She swung the door open. Morgan stood on the tiled porch, looking at the faded ceramic frogs and trolls under the prickly pear cactus near the door.

"Morgan?" Serena couldn't hide her disappointment.

"A hello would work fine." Morgan walked in confidently.

"What do you want?" Serena hated the way Morgan kept looking around her trying to see inside.

Morgan waved a twenty-dollar bill. "I want you to read the cards for me." She was still dressed the way she had been at school.

Serena stared at her.

"Please," Morgan pleaded more softly.

Serena shook her head. "The psychic shop is closed." But she gently pushed into Morgan's mind to find out why she had really come over. It was a mess inside, with half-completed thoughts and lots of worries. She always expected Morgan to be serene on the inside. That's what she projected outward. But it was only for show. Serena pushed around the surface thoughts, going deeper, trying to find a thought to hold on to and follow. Big speech at the prep rally on Thursday. Shopping. Credit card limit. Credit card limit?! Serena didn't even have a credit card. Then she found what she was looking for. Morgan liked

Collin. She more than liked him. No way did Serena want Collin to become one of Morgan's trophies.

"Serena." The word came to her softly at first. Then someone was shouting in her ear. Reluctantly, she left Morgan's mind.

"What happened to you?" Morgan rubbed her temples as if she had felt Serena inside her head. "You looked like you were in a trance or something."

"Just thinking."

"Well, will you read the cards for me?" Morgan snapped impatiently.

"Sure." Serena closed the front door as a plan came to her. It was wrong. She shouldn't. But she had to keep Morgan away from Collin.

"It's dark in here," Morgan complained.

"So turn on a light." Serena started down the hallway. She didn't want Morgan to see the smile on her face and get suspicious.

Morgan flicked on a light switch. A blaze of light sparkled from the chandelier hanging over the entrance. She followed Serena down the unlit hallway and through the dark dining room, turning on lights. Finally they pushed through a swinging door and entered the yellow kitchen, which smelled of freshly baked cookies.

Wally was curled on the table near the khaki pants Jimena had laid out. She was cutting the legs open up to the crotch so she could sew the panels together to make a long skirt.

"That's so gross," Morgan commented.

"What?" Serena wondered if Morgan was talking about the skirt Jimena was making.

"The raccoon," Morgan said with disgust. "They have diseases, you know, ones humans can catch."

"I take him to the vet every few months."

"It's probably against the law anyway."

"So what you going to do about it?" Jimena put down her scissors and stared at Morgan.

Wally seemed to sense the tension between them. He climbed off the table and scuttled flat-footed toward Morgan. She backed up, fanning the bottom of her coat to shoo him away.

Jimena laughed and Morgan glared at her.

Serena took the plate of cookies to the table. "Here, have one. I just made them."

Morgan looked at the cookies as if they were rat-poison. "No thanks." She carefully brushed off a chair before she seated herself.

Serena sat on the other side and shuffled the cards four times. She set the deck in front of Morgan. "Divide the cards into three stacks with your left hand."

Morgan looked at Jimena. "This is private, all right?"

"Sure." Jimena gave her a fake smile. She picked up the pants and left the room.

Morgan divided the cards into three stacks, but her eyes kept glancing at the back door as if she expected Collin to walk in any minute.

Serena took the cards and wondered what Morgan would do if she knew Collin was upstairs. Probably find a reason to go upstairs and accidentally stumble into his bedroom.

Serena flipped the first card and didn't bother to look at the face of the card.

"You're here about a guy," she announced as if she had read it in the card.

Morgan smiled and seemed impressed.

"Oh, no." Serena gasped as she turned the next card over.

"What?" Morgan immediately leaned forward. How could anyone look so perfect?

"He doesn't like you." Serena shrugged apologetically. Did he? In reality she didn't know how Collin felt about Morgan.

Something changed in Morgan's eyes then. Was she sad? Morgan? Serena actually started to feel sorry for her. She pushed back into Morgan's mind to see and found something that surprised her. Jealousy. Morgan was jealous of her? Serena Killingsworth? She examined the feeling closely, surprised by how much Morgan admired the way Serena dressed, and how she wished she were talented like Serena. Serena softened a little. She slowly left Morgan's mind and turned the next card. She started to say there was still a chance, but before she could, Morgan spoke.

"You know, Serena," Morgan chided, "you really should do something about the way you dress. It's a complete embarrassment to your brother."

Serena's mouth fell open. Was it? Had Collin told Morgan that? Frantically, she shoved back into Morgan's head and pushed through her thoughts, trying to find a memory of a conversation that Morgan might have had with Collin when he told her that Serena embarrassed him. When she didn't find it, she stopped and pulled away from Morgan's mind.

Morgan looked at her strangely. "Do you have any aspirin?" she asked.

Serena searched through the cupboards, then came back with two aspirin and a glass of water. She handed them to Morgan.

Morgan tossed the aspirin in her mouth and sipped the water.

Collin came back in the kitchen. He had changed into vans and khakis and the vintage rayon Hawaiian shirt with palm trees and beaches that Serena had bought him at Aardvark's.

"Hi, Collin." Morgan's headache seemed to have vanished miraculously. She crossed her legs, exposing a nice slice of tan thigh above her boots.

Collin was surprised to see her. Unhappy? No. He looked at Morgan with real joy. "Hey, whatcha been up to?"

Morgan looked at Serena. "I guess your cards got confused."

"What?" Collin asked.

"Serena was just trying to mess up my life." Morgan stood and started playing with the buttons on Collin's shirt.

"I just say what the cards tell me," Serena lied.

Morgan shrugged. "Don't worry about it. I'm so used to your jealousy that it doesn't even bother me anymore."

"*What?* I've never been jealous of you."

"Oh, please." Morgan waved her off. "It's so obvious, the way you look at me."

Serena looked from Morgan to Collin. She expected Collin to defend her but instead he looked at her as if she had disappointed him.

She knew she shouldn't do it. Maggie had taught her never to use her gift to her advantage, especially when it could hurt someone. Too bad. She rammed into Morgan's mind again, searching until she found the speech she was supposed to give at the pep rally on Thursday. With one tiny zap, the speech Morgan had worked so hard on was pushed behind the memory of her sixth-grade Christmas party, when she had stuffed her bra with Kleenex. Serena hadn't perfected this part of her power yet, so Morgan would probably remember some of her speech. But no way was she going deliver it with the usual smooth Morgan confidence. Serena backed out, satisfied.

Morgan rubbed her temples.

"You okay?" Collin seemed concerned.

"Just a bad headache." Morgan eyed Serena suspiciously. "I never get headaches."

Serena tried to hide the wicked grin that was stretching across her face. She picked up a cookie and bit off a piece.

Morgan continued to rub her temples. "Let's drive down to the beach." She looked at Collin. "Maybe I need fresh air."

"Sure." He stepped forward.

"Shouldn't you practice your speech?" Serena offered, stifling a laugh.

"What speech?" Morgan seemed baffled.

"I heard you were supposed to give one at the pep rally on Thursday," Serena said innocently.

Morgan looked reflective for a moment as if she were trying to pull some thought into focus. "I can't think right now."

They left and Jimena snuck back into the room. "Okay, what did you do?"

"How do you know I did anything?"

"You were all squinting and zombied out. I knew you were in her mind."

"Do you think Morgan noticed?"

"She's too self-involved. So what did you do?"

Serena suddenly remembered Maggie. "I'm in big trouble." Maggie was going to be so disappointed in her. "I zapped her mind. Not big, but enough. Let's just say that the pep rally will be very different this time."

Jimena smiled. "I'm down with that. They're always so boring. I can't wait."

"I shouldn't have done it. It's just that she makes me so mad."

"Don't worry about her. She's a *rata*."

"*Rata?* A rat?" Serena said.

"A girl who hangs around waiting for guys. She's got no life." Jimena looked at her watch. "I got to get over to Children's Hospital so I can get in enough hours this month. Sorry I can't stay longer."

"See you tomorrow." Serena waved.

After Jimena left, Serena sat in a chair and set her cello on the end pin between her knees. She loved the way she had to hug the cello when she played. She dreamed of meeting her idols some day in a master class or onstage, someone like Yo-Yo Ma or Han-Na Chang. She picked up her bow and began to play. The music flowed around her, sad and filled with longing.

She had only been playing for a little while when she looked up and gasped.

Zahi stood in the kitchen watching her.

"I am sorry," he apologized. "But your back door was open and I heard the cello music." He smiled. "It drew me to you as if it were calling me. It is quite lovely."

"Thank you." She wondered why she wasn't more upset that he had come into the house without knocking or announcing himself.

He pulled a chair up next to her. "I love the cello," he said shyly.

"Me, too," she agreed. "It communicates the way no other instrument can. It's so sorrowful and theatrical. It seems almost human the way it expresses so many emotions." She blushed and felt suddenly stupid for sharing her passion with him.

"It is you," he whispered, his voice solemn. She felt as if he were talking to her from a very deep place inside himself that he seldom shared. "The cello is only wood and a bow. You are the real instrument. It is your deep emotion that I hear when you play." He touched her cheek lightly.

"Thanks," she said, again feeling thrilled that they had shared so much.

"Play again," he asked. "Please."

She leaned over her cello. She started to play

with a long strong note, making sure the sound was even through the whole bow.

Then her fingers worked a fast run and she stepped into another world. The kitchen and Zahi were no longer there, only her music swirling around her until she was lost in it.

CHAPTER FIVE

SERENA SAT on a folding chair, put a
Tootsie Pop in her mouth, and waited nervously.
The gym had a stale smell left over from years of
basketball games. Sneakers caught and squeaked on
the polished wood floors as kids filed into the
room and talked noisily, waiting for the pep rally to
begin.

Finally, the lights dimmed and Morgan walked
across the stage, smiling at the football players seated on chairs behind her. She wore iridescent paisley-
print pants, a square-neck top, and lots of attitude.
Serena hated to admit it, but she looked good.

Morgan stepped behind the podium and bent the microphone to her. Then she paused and nervously twisted a strand of hair. She cleared her throat. Finally she began her speech. "The day of my Christmas party in sixth grade was the worst day of my life."

Kids in the audience looked at each other and shrugged. The football team seated behind her shifted uneasily.

"That was the day I stuffed my bra with Kleenex," she said too loudly, and made the microphone shriek.

"Woo-hoo!" someone shouted.

Some kids began to laugh. Coach Dambrowsky hurried across the stage, his heavy footsteps making loud thuds on the wood floor.

"The Kleenex fell out when I started dancing," Morgan continued seriously. "One piece came out, and then another, until finally I ran to the bathroom and emptied my bra."

Morgan looked up at the stage lights as if something had just occurred to her. "So don't stuff your bras with Kleenex. You may think guys don't like flat-chested girls, but I found out that day they do."

Guys hooted and applauded.

She started to speak again, but her words trailed off as Coach Dambrowsky took the microphone. "I think that was an interesting speech, Morgan, but let's introduce the football team now." He handed the mike back to Morgan.

She smiled nicely and glanced back at the football players, who were stretched out in their folding chairs. They grinned devilishly back at her. Some waved.

She paused for a long moment as if she were trying to remember something else. "I should have used socks," she continued. "But I was afraid they might start smelling." She cupped her hands under her breasts. "I'm glad I no longer have to worry about that or have to put up with being wedged in those padded bras."

Guys howled and whistled. The football team applauded.

Coach Dambrowsky grabbed the mike again. "Thank you, Morgan," he said nervously. "Why don't you have a seat, and I'll introduce the players."

Morgan took a seat, and even from the back of the auditorium Serena could see her blush bright red.

The kids in the gym were still laughing when Jimena, Serena, Catty, and Vanessa walked out into the sunlight.

"Why was Morgan talking about stuffing her bra?" Catty wondered.

"What did that have to do with getting us excited about a football game?" Vanessa added.

Jimena couldn't stop laughing. "Yeah, it made sense." Jimena glanced at Serena.

"You promised you wouldn't say anything!" Serena scolded.

"Cool." Catty looked at her with admiration. "What did you do to her?"

"You didn't!" Vanessa's eyes were wide. "I always knew she had stuffed her bra. I remember the party."

"Take us back in time so we can listen to her speech again," Jimena begged Catty.

"Let's go back to the party!" Catty's eyes dilated as if a potent energy were building in her brain. The minute hand on her watch started turning backward.

Serena caught her wrist. "It's not funny. I feel really bad about it."

"You should feel bad." Vanessa was being nice as usual. "The whole school heard her confess. She's going to be so embarrassed."

"Why should Serena feel bad?" Catty asked. "Morgan deserved it after everything she's done."

Michael Saratoga appeared behind Vanessa and put his arm around her. His wild black hair hung in thick curls on his shoulders, and a barbed-wire tattoo circled his upper arm. He had strong angular features, a great smile, and soft dark eyes. "Hey, you guys. Do you know why Morgan's speech was so crazy?"

"No!" they all shouted in unison.

Michael smiled. "Just asking."

Morgan stomped over to them, her neck and chest still pink with embarrassment "You witch!" she screamed at Serena.

Everyone turned and looked at her. "I know you did something to me, Serena."

"What's your trip?" Jimena stepped up to Morgan and started to push her away.

Serena grabbed Jimena's hands and held them.

Morgan glared at Serena. "Like I would go up onstage and tell the whole school about the most embarrassing day of my life. You did something!"

"What could I have done?" Serena tried to seem as sincere as she could.

"You can tell fortunes," Morgan stated. "So I bet you do more. You probably put a spell on me because your brother likes me! How else could I have forgotten my speech? I mean I told everyone about the Kleenex—" Morgan stopped. She glanced at Michael and her face turned a deeper red.

Everyone laughed except Serena.

"No one can put a spell on you, Morgan," Michael told her. "You were just doing what you always do."

"What?"

"Being totally self-absorbed."

"But I never forget my speech." Morgan put her hands on her hips.

"If Serena did something to you, you should be thanking her," Michael added. "It was the best pep rally we've had all year."

Morgan tilted her head. "You're right." She smiled at Serena but her eyes looked vengeful. "What am I thinking? Just nerves from giving a brilliant speech." She twirled and stormed away.

"Wow." Michael looked concerned. "I've never seen her so upset. You think she's having a breakdown? Maybe we should tell the school counselor."

"She's all right," Vanessa assured him, and glanced at Serena before she and Michael walked away.

"Don't let Morgan get to you," Catty soothed. "It was really funny what you did."

Serena caught her thoughts and knew Catty was going to repeat the pep assembly over and over.

"I'll meet you later at Chado's." Catty walked off.

When she left, Serena looked at her watch. "I've got to go or I'll be late for my cello lesson."

"Yeah, see ya," Jimena called.

Serena picked up her cello from the music room, then walked over to Bella's house for her lesson.

She had trouble with the fast runs and could hear Bella click her tongue impatiently every time she stumbled. But it was the shaky long note that made Bella touch the bow gently, signaling her to stop.

"Serena." Bella spoke in her thick Russian accent. "Do you know you are playing a cello? Did you think maybe it changed into a drum?"

"Sorry." Serena felt embarrassed.

Bella sighed heavily and sat beside her, her arms wrapping around Serena to show her how to position her fingers to play the multiple stops with which she was having difficulty.

When her hands fluttered away, Serena could still smell Bella's lilac powder. Serena played the measure again.

"Perfect." Bella applauded. She sat on the couch facing Serena. "Having a student like you, Serena, is one of the great joys in my life."

"But," Serena added for her.

"*But* an artist must surrender to her work, day after day, even on days when she doesn't want to practice, days when her mind is on boys and dances and dresses. Talent alone . . ." Her shoulders slumped as she sighed heavily. "A person with less talent will have more success if they practice, but they'll never be able to touch the soul the way you can, Serena. You can make people feel and long and appreciate—but it takes sacrifice."

She walked over to the window as if she were suddenly alone in the room, and looked out. Then she turned and looked back at Serena. "Don't fail yourself, Serena."

Twenty minutes later, Serena walked into Chado's. She loved looking at the brown canisters of tea that lined the walls in the front room. She peeked into the lavender room where tea was served. The room was crowded already. Then she saw Maggie sitting in a corner near the window. She really looked like a retired schoolteacher. Her long gray hair was curled in a bun, her delicate fingers ran up and down the handle on her teacup, and she was smiling at nothing in particular. She lifted her cup and took a sip.

Serena walked over to her and set down her cello beside the table.

Maggie stood and gave her a warm embrace.

Serena started to smile and stopped. Maggie was looking at her strangely.

"What is it, my dear?" Maggie touched Serena's cheek. "You seem so distraught."

"I . . ." She looked down. Daughters of the Moon were never supposed to use their powers to hurt others, and Serena had definitely done so in zapping Morgan, even if Morgan did deserve it. How was she going to tell Maggie? She didn't want to disappoint her.

Before she had a chance to explain what she had done, Jimena, Vanessa, and Catty walked in the front door.

"Hi." Catty sat down. "Did you tell Maggie about your dream yet?"

"No," Serena answered.

"What dream?" Maggie lifted her teacup and took a long sip.

"It was a really weird dream." Serena spoke slowly. "It was about a fire."

"Yeah," Jimena added. "Only it was cold."

"The flames were cold, but it still burned the wood," Serena explained.

"But not the girl who walked into the flames," Vanessa continued for her. "What was her name? Lecta?"

Maggie looked up sharply.

"What's wrong?" Serena leaned forward. Maggie was too powerful to let anyone into her mind, but her emotions shimmered in the air like an aura.

"Serena, dear," Maggie began, her concern visible on her face.

Serena clasped her shaking hands under the table. "Tell me."

"I'm afraid you've witnessed an arcane

ceremony of the Atrox." Maggie looked at them solemnly. "I wanted to discuss the new Followers, but this seems far worse. *Frigidus ignis.*"

"What's that?" Jimena asked.

"The Atrox gives immortality to favored followers who prove themselves, and"—she paused—"to Daughters of the Moon who turn to the Atrox and become Followers. The chosen ones step into the cold fire and the flames burn away their mortality and bestow eternal life."

Serena was thunderstruck. "It wasn't a dream?"

"But I went back," Catty protested. "I didn't see a fire."

"You couldn't see the fire." Maggie sighed. "The Atrox wouldn't allow you to see it unless . . ." She looked at Serena and fell suddenly silent.

"What?" Serena demanded.

"Lecta wasn't the girl's name," Maggie told them. "*Lecta* means 'chosen one'. *Lecta*, or *Lectus* if it is a boy. It is a very high honor to be chosen from the legion of Followers to receive one of the highest gifts the Atrox can bestow . . . immortality."

"You'd think people would have heard about the fire and all tried to jump in," Jimena mused. "I mean, *damn*, to live forever."

"It's not quite that easy." Maggie looked grim. "The Atrox must invite you into the fire. If not . . ."

"What?" Catty sipped her tea nervously.

"If you attempt to enter the fire, even brush a hand through it when you're not the chosen one—you suffer a horrible death."

Serena began to shudder. She had brushed her hand through the flames. What did that mean?

"But why would the Atrox allow me to witness such a ceremony, and not Catty?" Serena tried to keep her voice calm.

Maggie paused and shook her head. "It's such an ancient ceremony. I didn't realize it was still practiced."

Serena couldn't ease the disquieting feeling that was growing inside her.

Maggie placed a warm hand on Serena's. "You must be careful. The Atrox and its Followers can be very seductive. They could trick you into becoming one of them without using their powers of will."

"Am I a chosen one?" Serena could barely get the words out.

"Perhaps," Maggie answered her. "Perhaps the Atrox has chosen you."

A shiver spread through Serena.

Jimena looked at her. "We've got your back. We're not going to let anything happen to you."

Serena shook her head sadly. "Remember the tarot cards? The devil, the moon, and the high priestess? The cards predicted my fall."

"No," Maggie declared firmly. "You must never be fatalistic."

"But you made it sound like the Atrox doesn't let you see the fire unless—"

"No," Maggie interrupted. "I said the Atrox is very seductive. One of the powers of evil is to make you think your destiny is inescapable, but things are never hopeless."

The waitress brought over tiered silver plates with little sandwiches and pastries.

Maggie poured tea for each of them and began to speak quietly. "You must be very strong now. This new group of Followers is somehow connected to the cold fire, even though it was Stanton and the Hollywood group who showed the fire to Serena. Remember that there is much competition among Followers for a place of power in the Atrox hierarchy."

She glanced around her to make sure no one was listening before she continued. "Because the Daughters of the Moon live in Los Angeles it is only natural that ambitious Followers should find their way here, hoping to win the biggest prize— the seduction of a Daughter of the Moon or the theft of her powers. The Atrox would award such a deed by allowing the Follower into its inner circle."

She took a bite of scone and resumed speaking in hushed tones. "The Atrox is ruthless. It may very well have tricked Stanton into showing the fire to Serena in order to make her more vulnerable to the one who will try to convince her to step into the flames."

Serena stared at her tea. Did Maggie think she would ever betray the Daughters of the Moon?

Jimena took her hand and held it tightly.

Maggie seemed to read her thoughts. "People once thought that Hekate had betrayed her role and become an evil force, but that wasn't true."

"Who's Hekate?" Catty asked.

"The goddess of the dark moon," Maggie explained, and sipped her tea.

"If she's the goddess of the dark moon she must be evil," Vanessa surmised.

"Why would you think that?" Maggie seemed astonished. "Someone has to reign over the dark. That's when people need help the most, isn't it?"

"So Hekate was good?" Jimena looked hopeful.

"She did some very good things," Maggie hesitated. "But then . . ."

"But then what?" Catty was becoming impatient.

"Oh, I don't know, maybe she lived in the darkness too long."

They all looked at Serena, even Jimena. Did they think she was going to reign over the dark? Become a Follower?

Maggie continued, "Hekate portrays most vividly the struggle between good and evil that is in each one of us."

Serena felt suddenly ill at ease. She needed to do something. Her muscles were too tense and her hands and feet too jittery to stay seated at the table. She jumped up. "I'd better go."

"Please don't," Maggie said and looked at her kindly.

Serena tried to smile, but hot tears brimmed her eyes. She picked up her cello case and hurried outside.

She didn't slow down until she was at the corner of Third and La Cienega, waiting for the light to change. She stared across the street at the Beverly Center. The parking structure was aboveground to prevent methane gas seepage, a potentially lethal chemical hazard that existed in this part of Los Angeles. The mall took its odd shape because it curled around a working oil rig in back.

Someone called her name.

She turned. Zahi waved.

"Serena, what are you doing?" He ran up to her. "Daydreaming? I am glad you were, it gave me a chance to catch up to you."

She glanced at the light. It had turned green. Now the yellow-orange hand was flashing, warning pedestrians to stop.

Zahi took her cello and they ran across the street. Cars honked impatiently at them.

"You seem upset." Zahi looked concerned. "Is something bothering you?"

"It's nothing."

"Maybe you would like to talk with me about it, no? You will feel better if you do."

He took her hand. His touch surprised her. She looked into his eyes, so clear and intently watching her, as if she were the only person in the world who mattered to him. Suddenly Maggie's warning didn't seem very important. It was hardly the first time Serena had been in danger, anyway. Only last month she and Jimena had had to rescue Catty and Vanessa from the Followers. She could handle the Atrox. Of course she could. Why was she worried when such a cool guy seemed to like her?

"Do you need to go home right now?" He didn't take his hand away.

She shook her head. "No, Dad will be late. He's working on a big case and Collin is surfing."

"Good. Then please go with me to Michel Richard's for a cappuccino."

"Sure," she responded, even though her stomach was already full with tea and scones. She wanted to be with him.

"Great." He smiled and kissed her lightly on the cheek.

She sucked in her breath, startled by the kiss.

That's when she heard Jimena call her name.

"*Oye*, Serena, wait up!"

She looked back.

Vanessa, Catty, and Jimena darted through traffic as the cars started to roll forward. A barrage of horns and squealing brakes filled the air.

Zahi stepped back. "But you have plans with your friends. I should leave, no?"

Serena wanted to go with him, but more than anything she hated girls who dumped their friends to spend time with a guy.

"Yeah." She made an effort to hide her disappointment. "I guess so." Zahi walked away.

"He's so cute." Catty elbowed Serena playfully. "I love his accent. I wonder what France is like."

And suddenly they fell quiet, thinking about their final destiny when they turned seventeen.

"Yeah." Serena spoke quietly. "I wonder, too." It scared her if she thought about it for too long. She didn't want to lose her memories of any of their adventures. She looked at her friends. Did they have similar fears? They were fifteen now. The change was only two years away.

Vanessa was the first to break the dark mood. "Let's go over to the Skinmarket and try on makeup."

"Yeah!" Catty whooped.

They ran to the escalators and rode up to the seventh floor.

Serena stopped at the two-tone false eyelashes.

"You'll look like a *payasa*," Jimena warned, and picked up a pair with tiny red feathers.

"What's that?"

"A clown." Jimena laughed and took the eyelashes with the tiny feathers up to the cashier. "But a totally cool one."

Catty squealed. They all turned. She was holding up a can of hair spray and a stencil. "Look at this. We can spray hearts and lightning bolts on our hair."

"Do me," Jimena begged.

A few seconds later Jimena had a silver lightning bolt on either side of her head.

"Wild!" Serena grinned and tried to remember why she had been so worried when she ran out of Chado's earlier. Everything was perfect. She had great friends and a guy who really liked her.

CHAPTER SIX

FRIDAY NIGHT, Jimena and Serena strutted up to the line of kids waiting to go inside Planet Bang. Serena recognized some of the kids and waved. The fast rhythm of the music thumped through the walls and undulated around them, making them move their heads with the beat, but other things made Serena's heart jitter. She looked around hoping to see Zahi. The new lashes made a strange shadow at the top of her vision.

"Scope it out." Jimena nodded in the direction of the crowd. "You ever seen so many *churrisimos vatos*?" A sultry smile crossed her lips as she caught the sideways glances of the guys in line looking her over.

"I'm only looking for one."

"You're going to knock him out with those lashes." Jimena was still scanning the guys. "They're awesome and you know it."

Serena let a sly smile cross her face. She knew she looked good. She never cared if a guy liked the way she dressed. She loved the lashes and the glitter waves she'd painted on her bare legs. She'd spent the afternoon in Freddie's having extensions added to her hair. Now her black roots with the red tips had gorgeous tight curls that reached to her shoulders.

"Do you see him?"

Jimena shook her head. "You've got it bad."

"I can't believe I'm so nervous." Serena took a deep breath.

"Hormones." Jimena laughed. "It's not nerves. It's anticipation. You're dying to get your lips on his." The stenciled silver lightning bolts shimmered in her hair when she moved.

They both wore wide cuffs of sequins.

Jimena wore silver and Serena wore gold, to match their outfits.

"Maybe he's inside already." Serena stepped forward.

"Calm down," Jimena soothed.

At the door they opened their purses for security. A security guard with a gold tooth smiled and waved them inside to the cashier.

They paid and walked into the large interior that had once been a ballroom. The pulse of the music made the floor vibrate as machines on either side of the stage released mist into the room. The vapors caught the light show. Blue and red lasers pierced the air in time to the punk-rock beat.

They walked around the crowded dance floor. Guys turned and stared.

"I don't know why you're so nervous about Zahi, anyway," Jimena commented. "You could have your pick of the guys."

"Maybe," Serena answered with a big smile. "But Zahi's not just a guy. He is total perfection."

Jimena laughed.

The music stopped and the deejay hopped back and forth on the stage.

"Come on, raise the roof!" he shouted into a microphone. "Throw your hands up. Come on, raise the roof!"

Kids stopped dancing and lifted their hands to the ceiling in time to his cadence. He built the energy high and then let industrial music pump against the wall. The music took over and everyone started dancing. Jimena and Serena stood on the edge of the dance floor. The music beat through them and they started to move.

"I don't see him." Serena could feel her heart beating rapidly with anticipation as she scanned the dark corners and the dance floor.

"He'll be here!" Jimena rolled her eyes. "Let's stand in the light. I want to see what people think of my outfit."

They moved over to the canteen where a big guy with a buzz cut sold soft drinks and pretzels.

"Okay, ready? Get anything?" Jimena posed and put a dollar down for a Pepsi.

Serena concentrated. "Most of the guys are

thinking you're hot, but they don't want to ditch the girls they came in with."

Jimena was wearing a shimmery silver skirt and a halter top. "All right, I'm going to go bikini now." She tugged, then pulled the skirt below her belly. Her tattoos looked good and the hoop in her belly button sparkled as she aligned the hip-hugging skirt with her hipbones.

"You got their attention now." Serena laughed. *"Do you ever."*

"Okay, dig deeper." Jimena smiled big. "Are any of them wondering what I like to read?" She moved one hand sensually down her hip and rested it lightly on her thigh.

"Ah . . . no." Then Serena stopped. She was picking up something. Impossible. It sounded like Collin. *Jimena looks really good tonight.*

She shook her head. Collin was surfing or at home, no doubt, but still she found herself involuntarily scanning the kids in the club, looking for him.

"What?" Jimena watched her closely. "Did you find him?"

"Sorry, you didn't find Mr. Perfect tonight," she stated finally.

Jimena shrugged. "Maybe tomorrow."

The deejay was going back and forth between sounds—top forty, house, disco, and techno—until he saw what the kids would dance to, then he'd stay with that. He started another song and the strobe light flashed, making the room jump with the strange flicker of old film footage.

That's when she saw him. Zahi was walking toward her. He wasn't bagged out like the other guys. He wore a black T-shirt under a black leather jacket, and his hair was slicked back and parted in the middle, the sides starting to fall into his eyes.

She squeezed Jimena's arm.

"You gotta chill," Jimena said.

"I can't."

"Yeah, you can." Jimena pulled her onto the dance floor. "You're a goddess, remember? One thing you got is cool. Like an iceberg." She put her hands on Serena's hips and they started dancing, bodies flowing with the music, hips swaying.

"Make him want you," Jimena whispered. "Let him spend long, tortured nights dreaming about you."

"Look and suffer." Serena let her hands reach for the heavens. The tips of Jimena's fingers touched hers, and then she felt other hands on her waist. Her lungs took in a sharp breath. Her heart raced. She turned slowly. The hands held her waist more tightly. Zahi danced slow and sensual next to her. His jeans rubbed against her bare legs, and he pulled her closer and closer until their breath mingled. His eyes lingered, taking in every bit of her. Her heart throbbed until she couldn't draw a breath.

Jimena giggled behind her.

"See ya." Jimena waved and then there was only Zahi. Even the music seemed far away.

"I was afraid you wouldn't come." Zahi murmured the words against her ear like soft, lazy kisses.

Something stirred with delicious longing inside her.

"I had to wait until Jimena could get the

car," she explained, wondering if he could even hear her above the music.

"You look beautiful tonight," he said. His finger stroked her bare back.

Adrenaline shot through her and her heart pumped crazily.

"I'm glad you're here with me." He nestled his lips against the curve of her neck. His soft breath tickled her bare skin.

She closed her eyes and let her arms slowly entwine his neck. She had never been this close to a guy before. She didn't know it would feel this good. His lips moved up her neck to her cheek, searching for her lips.

Finally, she was going to have her first kiss.

She turned her face to him, her lips parting when someone tapped her shoulder.

Go away, Jimena, she thought.

The finger tapped again, hard and urgent.

She opened her eyes and angrily turned.

Collin stood behind her.

"Collin?" she said in shock. "What are you doing here?"

"What are *you* doing, you mean?"

"You always said Planet Bang was a place for wanna-bes and gremmies," Serena reminded him.

"Obviously." He was looking pointedly at Zahi.

Morgan ducked from behind Collin. "Hi, Serena." Morgan smiled smugly. She looked incredible as always, in a slinky black camisole with shimmering white capris and sleek tiger-print sandals, hair glittered and curled.

She threaded her arm through Collin's and held on possessively. "I was just telling Collin how you hexed me."

"She didn't hex you, Morgan," Collin corrected.

Morgan shrugged.

"Hexed?" Zahi laughed and looked at Serena. "Is she calling you a witch?"

"I didn't do anything." Serena was feeling flustered with her lie.

Suddenly, Jimena was beside her. "Are you still playing that tune?" Then she glanced at Collin. "And what are *you* doing here?"

Before Collin could answer, Morgan spoke. "I know she did something to me when I was over at her house. I don't get headaches."

"You think Serena's a *bruja*? A witch?" Jimena asked dangerously.

"Those things are possible," Morgan replied. "Scientists have studied curses and they're real. Right, Collin?"

Serena watched Collin closely.

He ignored Morgan and looked at Jimena. "So you know about witches and spells, Jimena? I bet you cast a lot of spells on guys."

"Yeah, well, you'll never know, will you?" Jimena snapped.

Collin smirked. "What makes you think I'd want to know?"

"That's right." Jimena nodded to Morgan. "You like girls all shiny and smiley."

"What does *that* mean?" Morgan knew she had been insulted, but wasn't sure how.

"If you have to have it explained to you, you're more *tonta* than I thought." Jimena crossed her arms in front of her chest.

The music changed to a sultry beat.

"This music is banging." Jimena started to sway. "I'm going to dance." She strutted out to the dance floor and two guys quickly walked up to her.

Collin took Morgan's arm. "Let's dance."

"Aren't you going to talk to your sister?" Morgan said.

Serena glanced at Collin expectantly.

"Come on." Collin took Morgan out to the dance floor near Jimena. Morgan pouted and refused to dance until Collin coaxed her, running his hands up and down her arms. When they finally did dance, his eyes kept drifting back to Jimena.

Zahi curled his arms around Serena. "Why does she think you did something to her?"

Serena sighed. "It's a long story,"

"Let's forget about Morgan, then." He gently pulled Serena out to the dance floor.

Zahi drew her to him, his touch frighteningly tender, the heat from his body warming hers. Her skin suddenly became feverish and supersensitive. The caress of his hands on her bare back was making her dizzy. They danced to the luxurious feel of the song, their faces close as if they were sharing secrets.

A couple jostled into them and she fell hard against his body. His arms tightened and kept her there.

The music became more frenzied. Kids around them danced wild with the beat, but they stood motionless, holding each other.

He bent his head. He was going to kiss her now. She closed her eyes.

The music stopped. The sudden silence felt cruel, and then the houselights came on. She opened her eyes. Her lips, parted expectantly, were inches from Zahi's mouth. He didn't let her go.

The deejay introduced Michael's new band. The drummer started marking the beat, then the rhythm guitar and lead guitar began to play. The singer grabbed the microphone and the band went full tilt into smooth, feel-good music. Kids crowded the stage.

Jimena came running back to Serena and Zahi. "Where's Vanessa? I thought she wanted to dance when Michael played."

"I don't know!" Serena shouted above the music.

Michael played bass guitar and sang a song he had written for Vanessa. When he finished the crowd went wild. Most of the kids started dancing again, unable to resist the beat of the music.

Vanessa and Catty ran up to them. Like Serena and Jimena, they wore hip-hugging skirts, halter tops, and thick cuffs.

"Let's show them our moves," Vanessa said excitedly. She had been waiting to impress Michael with how well she had learned to dance.

Serena looked at Zahi questioningly.

"Please, I want to see you dance also."

"Wait for the next song." Jimena motioned to the band. "We need a different beat."

Then the music changed and the lead singer's voice belted a song with hungry desire. They were ready. They looked at each other, smiled, and melted together in a slow-moving swing that made everyone turn and stare, even Morgan.

Serena watched Zahi watching her; his eyes lingered, taking his time. She slid her body next to Jimena's, never taking her eyes off him. Then she bent lower, the long muscles of her thighs pulling tight. Rolling her hips with the beat, she placed her hands on Vanessa's shoulders.

Zahi smiled, his eyes half closed, and a jolt of pleasure shivered through her. She turned her head from side to side, moving as one with Jimena, Catty, and Vanessa. They slithered together. She turned back. Zahi had taken a step closer as if he needed to wrap his arms around her and hold her tight.

The music ended too soon. The lights came up and everyone applauded wildly. Girls bumped around Serena, crowding toward the stage to get autographs from the band members.

Serena continued to look at Zahi with sweet longing.

"Do you see that?" Vanessa asked with a flare of jealousy. "Look at all the girls who want autographs!"

The mood was broken and Serena turned slowly away from Zahi.

Catty giggled. "Don't look at the girls lined up for autographs, listen to the ones talking about you."

Girls were pointing at Vanessa and their voices carried over the crowd.

"That's Michael Saratoga's girlfriend," one said enviously.

"Isn't she pretty?" another added.

Vanessa beamed.

Jimena shook her head and laughed as more girls pushed toward Michael.

A girl lifted her sweater and asked him to sign her belly. He took a large black felt marker and scrawled "Michael" across her stomach. Other girls wanted him to sign arms and neck.

"Do you believe what he's doing?" Vanessa's anger flared up again.

"It's becoming a Michael-fest," Serena commented, and she felt Zahi's hand rest on her shoulder.

"You looked very good," Zahi whispered in her ear. "More than good."

"Thanks." Serena looked into his eyes.

Jimena nudged her. "Catch what's happening now?"

The next girl in line smiled coyly at Michael, then she undid the buttons on her blouse and stuck her chest out.

"What's she doing?" Vanessa's face was flushed.

Michael smiled sheepishly, then gripped the black felt marker and wrote his name over the swell of her breast. The girl touched the tips of his fingers when he finished writing and kept his hand there while she said something to him.

"What's she saying?" Vanessa asked.

"Forget about it," Jimena said. "You know Michael doesn't like her."

"What are they saying?" Vanessa insisted. Serena could feel Vanessa's anger like a sudden thunderclap resounding in her head.

"Just chatter," Serena lied. The girl was asking Michael to meet her later, but Michael said no.

"Look at me." Vanessa spoke tensely. "It's happening."

Serena turned. Vanessa was disappearing. Strong emotions made her lose control of her molecules. Her hands looked fuzzy.

"Help me," she whispered. Her greatest fear had always been that someone would see her disappear.

"Cover her," Jimena ordered. "She's going!"

Serena looked nervously at Zahi. Luckily he was staring at the commotion onstage.

"Relax," Catty coaxed, and swerved in front of Vanessa. "That girl's not his type. You're his number one."

Vanessa's hands and feet had vanished now and the side of her face had elongated into a funnel of dots. Her eyes were glassy and her voice sounded rubbery when she spoke, "How could he?"

"It's a guy thing," Jimena said. "Haven't you figured that out by now? You want to go invisible? Michael will see."

The girl turned and walked away from Michael, then looked back over her shoulder at him.

"He's still looking at her," Vanessa complained, but it was difficult to understand her now.

"Looking at her because he's so glad he's with you," Catty chattered on, trying to distract her. "Sing something, quick. It'll help you relax."

The girl waved to Michael, then blew him a kiss.

"That—" Before Vanessa could call the girl a name her voice left her.

"Do something," Jimena urged Serena. "See if you can zap her emotion. Quick! Go in and calm her!"

Serena had never tried to change someone's emotion before, but it was definitely going to be bad news if Vanessa disappeared and someone saw. She quickly pushed into Vanessa's mind. The anger was hot and thick and made it hard to enter. Her pinging molecules showered Serena like a barrage of searing needles.

Serena tried to calm Vanessa. Then she felt a crack in the anger and entered, hoping to pull a better emotion to the front of her mind, but behind the barrier of anger was a single thought that shocked Serena.

She burst from Vanessa's mind and took two staggering steps backward as if the thought had shoved her. She looked at Vanessa. How could one of her best friends think that about her? Did Catty and Jimena feel the same way?

CHAPTER SEVEN

ZAHI CAUGHT HER. "What is wrong?" he asked. "Are you feeling ill?" His brown eyes looked distressed.

"Nothing." She shook her head. But she was sweating now and couldn't stop her hands from shaking. Did Vanessa really think Serena would betray the Daughters of the Moon?

"You are shaking," Zahi whispered, and held her tightly.

She tried to pull away from him. "I'm not feeling very well," she said. "Maybe I should go home."

"Let me take you home, then," he offered.

"No." She spoke too sharply and pushed away from him.

He looked bewildered.

The houselights went down and the music started again. Kids crowded onto the dance floor and the strobe light flashed, making everything surreal. Michael ran to Vanessa and kissed her.

"Hey," Michael greeted her. "Seeing all those girls made me so happy I'm with you."

"Why?" Vanessa was still annoyed. He didn't seem to notice the way Vanessa's molecules had suddenly snapped back together when he touched her, or maybe he thought it had only been the lighting that had made her look so strange.

Serena watched them, her heart beating rapidly as she twisted into Vanessa's mind to see if there was more.

Michael smiled and answered Vanessa. "Because I know you'd never do something as crazy as ask a strange guy to sign your belly or . . . well, you saw, you know." He kissed her lightly.

"You didn't have to sign . . . where you signed," Vanessa said, but her anger was fading. Michael held her closely.

"I'm so glad I have you," he whispered. "You're not even jealous."

"Right." Catty winked at Vanessa.

Vanessa smiled, happy again, and her mind slowly closed, hiding her thoughts from Serena.

Serena tried to enter Catty's mind and see if she felt the same as Vanessa. Catty looked at her as if she sensed Serena's struggle to read her thoughts.

Serena stepped back, suddenly too dizzy and weak to stay inside. She turned back to Zahi. "I'm sorry, but I've got to leave. Jimena will give me a ride home."

His smile crumpled. He didn't bother to hide his disappointment or the concern he felt. "Call me tomorrow and let me know if you are feeling better."

She nodded and walked over to Jimena. "Take me home."

"What's up?" Jimena seemed uneasy.

"Can we just go now?"

Vanessa, Catty, and Jimena stared at her with worried expressions.

"Sure." Jimena didn't hesitate. They started walking toward the door.

Outside, she tried to push into Jimena's mind, but it was like a stone wall.

"What is it you don't want me to see?" Serena demanded.

"What do you mean?" Jimena dug the car keys from her purse.

"You know what I mean."

Jimena was silent. Her lips tightened.

"I thought you said we were always going to keep it real," Serena pleaded. "Always real between you and me."

Serena sensed that it was difficult for Jimena to tell her what was on her mind.

"I had a premonition," Jimena started slowly.

Serena waited. Her heart beat rapidly.

"I saw you standing in the cold fire," Jimena whispered. "That's what we've all been hiding from you. We didn't want you to worry."

"You should have told me." Fear trembled through Serena's body.

"We're watching over you," Jimena assured her. "We'll make sure it doesn't come true."

"But you've never been able to stop any of your premonitions from coming true."

Jimena was silent for a long time and when she finally spoke her voice broke. "I know," she said sadly.

CHAPTER EIGHT

SERENA LAY ON HER BED, twisting her leopard-print sheets around her and watching the slow-moving yellow globs in her purple Lava lamp. She tried to take in deep, soothing breaths, but her anxiety was like heavy stones crushing her chest and she couldn't expand her lungs. A deep cold had settled inside her. She tossed and stared at the corners of the room, wondering if another light might help.

When she was young she had believed in witches, vampires, and ghouls. After her mother left, she slept with all the lights on. That's what

◄ 141 ►

she had missed most when her mother had gone: safety in the night. Now her childish fears were back to haunt her, but with a new and real focus. Evil did lurk in the night and she could even name it. The Atrox.

There was no way she could betray the Daughters, was there? She couldn't imagine becoming a Follower.

Wally jumped on her bed, startling her. He snuggled his way under the covers and curled in a ball next to her.

"What do you think, fur face?" she said, and scratched behind his ear. His masked face stared back from beneath the covers as if he were trying to comfort her. She pulled him against her and finally she was able to drift into an uneasy sleep.

She awoke a few hours later with a start, her heart beating rapidly. If it had been a dream that awakened her, she couldn't remember it. She shook her head and sat up in the bed.

Wally scooted deeper under the covers.

Soft music came from downstairs. Maybe Collin was home already. She glanced at her clock.

It was only 11:45. She didn't think Morgan would release him that early. Still she jumped from bed, slipped into her furry slippers, and hurried into the hallway and down the stairs. She needed to talk to him. He had a way of making her feel safe and comfortable. She couldn't tell him the truth, but just talking to him would help ease the tension.

A light shone from under the door in her father's den, and music was coming from the CD player. She listened. She didn't think Collin would be listening to Mozart's *Requiem Mass*. Could her father be home? He said he'd be in San Francisco all weekend. Maybe the music was Morgan's idea of romance. Collin would be playing surf guitar music by Dick Dale and his Del-Tones.

Cautiously, she stepped forward and pressed her hand against the door. If Morgan was sitting with Collin on the couch, she was going to back away. She peeked into the den, then froze, gasping involuntarily.

Terrified, she took three quick step backward, turned, and ran.

CHAPTER NINE

STANTON LEANED AGAINST the
leather sofa, leafing through a book on medieval
architecture. His blue eyes glanced at her with hot
energy, and a dangerously sensual smile slid across
his face. He tossed the book aside and ran after her.

She ran back up the stairs, her footsteps
thundering through the house. Where was all her
goddess power? Normally her nerves would be
thrumming and power surging through her. But
tonight her mind was too jangled from everything
that had happened. What could she do? A 911
call was a silly idea. What would she say?

His feet pounded on the steps behind her, gaining.

She could stop and face him, but she had to compose herself first. She rushed to her room, slammed the door and locked it. He smashed into the door.

She tried to calm herself and build her energy.

He continued to bang against the door, and then silence followed.

She glanced at the door. The doorknob started to turn. Then suddenly it snapped, the lock broke with a loud clank, and Stanton stepped into her room.

She took in a deep breath. Power gathered in her chest and then spread with force to the tips of her fingers. Her moon amulet cast a silvery glow across the room.

"Is that what you wear to bed?" Stanton smiled at her. "I had expected something a little more edgy."

"What I wear to bed?" She looked down at her pajamas, then glanced back at him and shook her head. This had to be a dream.

"You're not dreaming," he corrected her. The light from the moon amulet shot across his face. He blinked, then with a swiftness that seemed impossible his hand shot out and grabbed her.

She tried to pull free. When she couldn't, she pushed into his mind to stop him, but he had already invaded hers. He wasn't trying to battle her. He was soothing her, his calming words whispering around her anxiety and fear with the softness of angel wings.

"Serena." He repeated her name luxuriously as if he enjoyed the easy roll of it across his tongue.

"I can feel your heart beating fast," he continued. "But you don't need to be afraid of me. Look at me." The silky command in his voice made her want to gaze into his eyes. But that was too dangerous. He could trap her in one of his memories forever.

He pulled her to him with a gentleness she could never have expected from someone so evil. A delicious craving ran through her. She should hate his touch, but it was somehow drawing her to him.

And then against her will she opened her eyes. Had he made her do that? No, she had done it on her own. She was remembering something that was far away and she couldn't bring it into focus yet.

"I'm sorry." He spoke in hushed tones. "I know this is frightening for you. Every time I warn you, Zahi erases my warnings from your memory."

Confusion rolled through her. "Zahi?" She pulled back and stared into his soft blue eyes, even though that was the most dangerous thing she could do.

"Yes."

He had to be telling her lies to bring her defenses down, and then when she was no longer protecting herself he would attack.

She let her power build.

A lazy smile crossed his face. Couldn't he feel her preparing for battle? Wasn't he going to defend himself?

He spread his arms to his sides, smiled broadly, opened his mind to her, and waited for her attack. Another trick?

"You have the power to look into my mind and see if I'm telling the truth," he offered.

She watched him, not sure what she should do.

"I'm waiting."

What would she find if she penetrated his mind? She took a deep breath. Would he ensnare her? She plundered in and was met with a memory of the two of them walking along the beach on a chilled and foggy night, talking. It was the night of the cold fire. He held her hand. She pushed in farther and found a jarring memory of her fall from the bluff, the terrible seesaw sensation of teetering on the ledge and his struggle to pull her up. He had saved her. And finally she had willingly allowed him into her mind to remove the memories of the hour they had spent together so that he could find out who was stealing her memories and why.

She caught a glimpse of something else, but before she could examine it he jerked it from her with such force that she stumbled from his mind. The impact almost made her fall backward.

Stanton steadied her and they sat on the edge of her bed.

"That night at the beach." His words were soothing. "When you saw the cold fire. I came to you and you ran from me and fell off the bluff. That's how you broke your glasses and scratched your hands. You were caught on a ledge and I helped you up."

"The bruises on my arm?" she asked.

"From pulling you up," he explained. "I'm sorry." He touched her arm as if he were trying to take away the pain.

"You didn't trust me then, and you don't now." Stanton pulled something from his jacket pocket and handed it to her. Her blue sandals.

She looked at them. Spots of black tar stuck to the soles, and the purple-and-blue beadwork across the straps was covered with sand.

"That night at the beach, I knew someone was stealing your memories, so I erased the hour we'd spent together until I could find out who was stealing your memories and why. I suspected Zahi was pushing your memories deep into your unconscious so you couldn't remember my warnings."

"Zahi?" she asked in disbelief.

"Only the most powerful Followers can steal both memories and feelings."

"But why would you warn me?" She shook her head. This was impossible. "You'd want to see me destroyed."

"Zahi is my worst enemy," Stanton said with a flare of hatred. "And if he can deliver you to the Atrox, he wins a place of power above me."

She stared down at the carpet. If Stanton could deliver her to the Atrox he would also win a place of power.

"Yes," he answered her thoughts. "But I won't."

"How can I trust you and not Zahi if you're both Followers?"

"Because I haven't stolen your thoughts or memories."

"I don't know that." Could she believe him? Her sworn enemy was asking her to trust him, and she liked Zahi so much.

Stanton stood, suddenly full of rage. Or was it jealousy? She wasn't sure.

"Zahi is a master of deceit." He stomped back and forth across the room. He ran his hand through his blond hair. "He's like a chameleon. He can mold his personality to show you only the person you want to see. And he means to destroy you. I swear that is his only intent."

She chewed on her lower lip.

"I'll protect you," Stanton promised.

"I can't trust you," she insisted. "This is just another trick. You must have the same plans for me. Maggie told me about the Regulators. You wouldn't take such a risk."

Was it a look of surprise on his face, or fear? The Regulators were a small group who had the power to terminate any Follower who betrayed the Atrox.

"I haven't done anything to displease the Atrox," he said in a low voice, and then opened his mind to her. She couldn't believe what she saw there. Before she could be sure, the back door opened downstairs.

"That's Collin." She panicked. "He can't see you!"

"Don't tell me you're afraid of your own brother?" Stanton seemed to think that was funny. She hated the smirk that crept over his face.

She shoved him. "You want Collin to kill you? Hide."

That made him laugh louder. "Kill me?"

"Stop it," she warned him, "or he'll hear you."

"You think I should be afraid of your brother? I'm an immortal."

Collin's heavy steps filled the downstairs hallway. Her heart raced. Why was life so complicated?

His footsteps started up the stairs.

Stanton sat on the bed smiling at her.

"Please!" she begged. "He'll never understand."

Stanton didn't move.

"Serena?" Collin called from the hallway. "Are you still up?"

Her heart fell. How was she going to explain Stanton to her brother?

▼

CHAPTER TEN

"**I** CAN EXPLAIN," Serena said quickly as Collin stepped into her bedroom.

"Explain what?"

"The guy. He's a friend from school," she lied. "He needed a homework assignment. I—"

Collin pushed around her.

"Don't hit him!" She grabbed Collin's arm.

"Who?" Collin looked back at her.

She turned and looked into the bedroom. The room was empty. Maggie had told her some of the Followers were shape-changers. Was Stanton one? She let out a long sigh, and just as quickly new anxiety filled her. Maybe it had only been a dream. It had felt like one.

Collin looked at her strangely and placed a heavy hand on her shoulder. "You know, sometimes your weird jokes aren't very funny." There was true concern in his voice and she could feel the beginnings of one of his brotherly lectures.

"Not tonight, Collin," she said. "I don't need a big-brother lecture right now. . . ."

"I'm just worried about you," he continued. "You know, maybe Morgan is right. I mean, if you're making up having a guy in your room, maybe you really do need a boyfriend."

She was too tired to deal with this right now. She poked into his brain, took his worries about her and pushed them behind his memories of the North Shore on Oahu. Then she pulled out, blinked, and glanced at him.

He looked a little stunned.

"You were saying?" she asked.

"Can't remember what I was saying."

"You were telling me good night." She gave him a sweet sisterly smile.

"Yeah." A dreamy look covered his face. "You think maybe dad will take us back to Hawaii for Christmas?"

"Maybe, if we both ask him," she offered.

"Mmmm." He started out the room. At the door, he stopped and turned back. "Hey, I remembered what I wanted to tell you."

Her heart sank.

"You looked really good dancing tonight. Everyone said so. You and Jimena were awesome."

"Thanks."

When his bedroom door closed, she shut her door and leaned against it.

Stanton emerged from the shadows.

"So your brother thinks you need a boyfriend?" he teased.

"Stop."

"I wish I could have seen you dance tonight." His dangerous beauty was hypnotizing. She felt sorry for him suddenly, remembering what Vanessa had seen when she had been sucked into his memories. His father had been a great prince of Western Europe during the thirteenth century and had raised an army to go on a crusade against the Atrox. The Atrox had stolen Stanton to stop his father. She looked at him now and sensed the young, frightened boy he had once been.

"I have one last question," she began. "Why did I stay so long with you if all you needed to do was warn me about Zahi?"

An odd look crossed his face. "Look," he pulled her to him again. "Look in my eyes and I will show you." His hand brushed her cheek and then he held her face tenderly.

Did she dare?

"Zahi has stolen more than my warnings," he continued. "He also stole the memories of all the times we have spent together."

The words hit her with the power of a lightning strike. "You said *we*? Of the time *we've* spent together?"

"Yes, *us*," he whispered. "Let me show you. Just one memory for now. Later the rest."

Against her will, she fell deep into his thoughts. His memories swept around her. She tried to pull her mind back, but part of her was rushing to meet him as if she had waited a long time to do this. The sudden eagerness frightened her. What was happening? He was her enemy. She had done battle with him.

Despite herself, she was sinking deeper and deeper into the memories. Suddenly, she was reliving the hour they had spent together walking on the beach and talking. How could she have spent time with Stanton and not remember? Could Stanton really like her, his sworn enemy?

He looked into her eyes. She knew she should stop him, but her body shivered pleasurably with the feel of his warm lips on her neck. She finally let herself go and breathed in the sweet soap smell of him. Her lips moved slowly across his cheek to meet his, her desire irresistible.

He stared down at her as if he needed to savor this forbidden moment. He didn't bother to hide the eagerness in his eyes. With his hands, he cupped her face, sending a delicious shiver through her. Then his eyes closed and he kissed her, his lips soft on hers.

Her lips parted as if they had kissed him

before and then his tongue brushed lazily across her lips.

Too many dangerous emotions swirled around her. She felt disgust with herself for wanting him so desperately. She tried to stop the aching need that spread through her body. It was her mission to protect people from Followers. From Stanton. She couldn't allow herself to like him.

She stopped abruptly and looked up at him.

"You can't fight it," Stanton said.

Did he too think she would betray her destiny? How could she trust him? In the past he had deceived and betrayed Vanessa.

Stanton looked at her and she knew he was reading her distrust.

"I appreciated the kindness Vanessa showed me, but I never felt the connection with her that I feel with you. I've liked you since the first time our minds met in combat. I've more than liked you, Serena." His hand touched her cheek.

She remembered that battle. How strange it had been. She had suspected even then that he had been teasing and playful, not really trying to destroy her.

She shook her head.

"I'm telling you the truth," he insisted.

She felt hot tears gather in her eyes. He was telling the truth. But their kind of relationship would always be forbidden.

"That night when we walked on the beach you told me you were willing to risk it. You promised to defy everyone to be with me."

She gazed into his eyes and knew he was still hearing the doubt in her mind.

He turned and left.

CHAPTER ELEVEN

MONDAY MORNING Serena and Jimena
stood in line waiting to go through the metal
detectors. The high school had just banned back-
packs and messenger bags to stop kids from
smuggling drugs and guns onto campus.

Security guards asked guys in bagged-out
sweatshirts and jeans to lift their tops.

"Do they really think that if a guy is strap-
ping he's going to hide the gun in his waistband?
Get real." Jimena sniffed contemptuously. She
wore the khaki skirt she'd made from her slacks,
and a flirty, off-the-shoulder T.

Jimena took a sip of coffee from her Styrofoam cup. "Here. Want some?" She offered the cup to Serena.

Serena shook her head. She felt uncomfortably warm in her pink snakeskin jacket. The wooden platforms with the neon-green straps and rhinestones were already starting to cramp her toes.

"What's wrong?" Jimena asked finally.

"What do you mean?"

"You've been huffing and sighing all morning like you're still mad at me for keeping the premonition from you."

"No, it's . . ." She broke down and told Jimena about Stanton's visit, but she couldn't tell her everything, especially not about the memories of the time she and Stanton had spent together.

"Since when does a Follower care enough to warn one of us?" Jimena sipped the coffee.

"He said Zahi was a Follower."

Jimena laughed. "Zahi is about the sweetest guy I've ever met."

"Still. What if?"

"Zahi doesn't look like the new Followers. He's not all punked out. Look at his left arm. No tattoo. Stanton was playing with your mind. But if you're still worried, why not use your moon amulet?"

"I've looked at it. It doesn't glow when he's around."

A puzzled look crossed Jimena's face, and then it was her turn to step through the metal detector. She did and waited for Serena on the other side.

Serena passed through and then paused while one of the security guards went through her purse.

The guard handed the purse back to her and she caught up to Jimena.

"I'm talking about the power that Maggie just told us about," Jimena whispered. "The special one."

"What special power?" Serena asked as they walked toward their lockers.

"*De veras*, you don't remember?" Jimena sounded perplexed.

Serena shook her head.

"What's up with you lately? You were so psyched to try it out."

"Maybe it's the winter concert." Serena sighed. "Maybe algebra. My mind feels like mush."

"Maybe it's Zahi." Jimena giggled. "You're too in love to think about anything else."

"I don't know." Serena wondered what else she might have forgotten—or had pushed from her mind.

"Give Zahi your moon amulet to hold. If he's a Follower as Stanton says, then the moon amulet will leave a mark in his skin."

Serena clasped her amulet. How could she have forgotten something so important? She vaguely remembered Maggie telling them, but it felt far away and dreamlike.

"Here he comes now," Jimena said under her breath.

Serena turned. Zahi ran up to her. She took an involuntary step backward and smiled nervously. Could he really be stealing her memories?

The bell rang.

"Gotta go," Jimena called and ran off.

"Hello, Serena," Zahi said, and ignored the crowd of kids running to class. He wrapped his arms around her. "Let's leave school this afternoon, just you and me."

Serena hesitated. "You mean cut classes?"

"Yes."

A funny feeling crawled through her stomach. She glanced down at her amulet. Why wasn't it glowing? Or did it only glow when she was in danger? She couldn't quite remember. She looked into his warm brown eyes, then down at his perfect full lips.

"Sure," she finally said. "After algebra."

"I'll meet you at Borders in the coffee bar."

"Okay."

Two hours later, Serena hurried up the stairs in Borders. She sat in a chair next to the window and looked down at the traffic on La Cienega. She took a deep breath and leaned back. People were reading at the tables around her. Their thoughts combined into a soothing murmur, like the rush of water around stones in a creek. Her muscles began to relax. Only then did she realize how anxious she had felt.

Zahi came in and set his books on the table. "Campus security was watching the area between the gym and the music room. Sorry I'm so late. I'll get us something to drink."

He went to the coffee bar and came back with two steaming cups of chai tea and a chocolate chip muffin.

She breathed in the scent of ginger, clove, and cinnamon spices and looked through the steam across the table at Zahi.

Zahi reached over and took her hand. "I'm glad you came," he said and kissed the tips of her fingers. "You seem like a very serious student. I was afraid you wouldn't meet me."

She unhooked her moon amulet from the chain around her neck and handed the charm to Zahi.

"What is this?" He took it in his left hand. "A gift from another boy, perhaps?"

She laughed, all her doubts vanishing. "No,

not from a guy." She looked at his sweet smiling face. Zahi, a Follower? No way. How could she have ever suspected something so ridiculous? It seemed foolish to make him hold her amulet. Stanton's accusations felt more treacherous than true. She tried to remember what he had said exactly, but it was all so shadowy now.

Zahi rested his hand with the amulet under the table and sipped his tea. "So how is your practicing with the cello?"

"Okay." She started to feel at ease and more self-confident. "I'll have the sonata memorized by the winter concert."

"Good, I want to hear it. Promise to play it for me soon."

"I promise," she answered. The longer she was with Zahi, the farther the night with Stanton drifted into the unconscious layers of her mind.

"There is going to be a rave in the desert this Saturday night," Zahi said.

"I've always wanted to go to one." Serena smiled. "It sounds so cool, dancing all night."

"Go with me, then," he urged. "Can you

leave your house without anyone knowing?"

"I think so." She was getting excited. "Collin won't check on me, and Dad's working strange hours right now. Jimena will freak out. I know she's always wanted to go to one, too. I can't wait to tell her."

"Serena." Zahi was suddenly serious.

"What?"

"Without all your friends." He spoke softly. "They are very nice. I don't mean anything against them, but I want to spend time with you. Alone. Will you go out with me, Serena, alone?"

Her heart careened against her stomach. She hoped he didn't see how happy she felt.

He leaned across the table and whispered, "It should be a very romantic night. The moon will be full."

"Yes." She nodded. "I want to go."

"Good." He looked into her eyes. "I'll be at your house at seven, then, or do I need to meet you someplace?"

"No, come to the house. I'll get rid of everyone before you get there."

"Good," he said. Then he leaned completely across the table and kissed her quickly on the cheek. "I must go now." He stood and handed her necklace back to her.

She held it in her hand. She had forgotten that she had given it to him.

Serena quickly clasped it around her neck and immediately felt a sense of relief.

CHAPTER TWELVE

SATURDAY NIGHT, Jimena walked into Serena's room carrying a brown paper bag filled with cartons of takeout Chinese food. The aroma of green onions, garlic, and pork filled the room. Jimena set the bag down on the floor in front of the TV and flipped a video into the recorder.

Serena cleared her throat. "I . . . I think I'm coming down with flu or something."

"You stay in bed. I'll sit on the floor." She handed Serena a white carton of chop suey and a pair of chopsticks wrapped in paper.

"I think I just want to sleep," Serena tried again.

Jimena took the remote and put the movie on pause.

"Sorry," Serena apologized. "Maybe you should go."

There was so much disappointment in Jimena's face that Serena almost told her to stay. Guilt weighed heavily on her now. She couldn't believe she was lying to her best friend over a guy. If she did tell Jimena about the rave, she'd probably help her dress in something really funky and not even feel jealous. So why couldn't she bring herself to tell her?

"I can tell you're not feeling well," Jimena finally said.

"How's that?" Serena asked.

"You don't seem like yourself. All week you've been, I don't know, distant or something. You got a fever?" Jimena touched her forehead and a peculiar look crossed her face.

"What?"

"Nothing," Jimena said quickly, but Serena

knew she was holding something back.

She tried to peek inside her mind, but the wall was up again.

"Tell me. What did you see?" Serena insisted.

"I said *nothing.*" Jimena ejected the cassette from the recorder. She gathered the food and the videos together.

"Why are you upset?"

"I better go so you can get some sleep." Jimena left the room.

"Jimena," Serena called after her. She ran to the hallway but Jimena was already bounding nosily down the stairs.

She heard Jimena and Collin in the kitchen.

"Leaving so soon?" Collin asked.

"Yeah," Jimena said flatly. "You like Chinese?"

"Love Chinese," Collin answered. "Don't you want to share it?"

The back door opened with a squeak, and then Jimena yelled back as if she had stopped at the door remembering something.

"Check on your sister, okay?"

"Is she sick bad?"

"Just check on her," Jimena told him, and then the door banged shut.

Serena hurried back to bed and pulled the covers around her.

A few minutes later Collin's slow steps beat on the stairs. Finally he walked into her room holding a white carton and chopsticks. He picked a carrot with the chopsticks and tossed it into his mouth.

"You okay?" Collin asked.

"Sure, just a cold."

He sat on the edge of her bed. "Should I stay home and make you some chicken soup?"

"No, I'm just going to sleep. Go surfing. I'll be fine."

"Sure?"

She nodded.

He remained sitting on her bed eating chop suey as if he had something more to say. His words surprised her. "Has Jimena got a boyfriend?"

"No."

"Figures," he muttered and stood. "Get better. I'll check on you when I get home."

"No!" she said too loudly.

He turned and looked at her with concern.

"I mean, please don't. I need the sleep."

"Sure." He stood and left her room. She jumped up and waited by her bedroom door until she heard Collin leave through the back door. Then she ran to the window to make sure. She watched his utility van back out of the drive and turn down the street.

Serena went to the bathroom and locked the door. She stared at her reflection. Her eyes had a dark haunted look and the wide-eyed stare of an insomniac. Why wasn't she excited? Strange thoughts and feelings kept whispering across her mind. Was there something important she should be remembering? For some reason, her mind couldn't focus. She took foundation and dabbed it on the bluish circles under her eyes.

A picture of Stanton flashed across her mind with such startling clarity that she froze for a moment. He had visited her in her bedroom. Had that been a dream?

She put on mascara, pasted a bindi on her forehead, then pushed her hair back with a jeweled tiara. She liked the look with her new extensions.

She walked back to her room, looking for comfortable shoes. She could wear thick socks with her new Doc Martens. She found the shoe-box under her bed and pulled it out. What she saw inside made her hands start shaking.

The Doc Martens had been worn. When had she worn them before? She clutched them close to her chest and stared out the window, try-ing to focus on the memories from the back of her mind.

The full moon started to rise and with it came another memory of Stanton. She was find-ing it impossible to concentrate on anything. Had he warned her about something?

Normally the milky light from the moon made her feel strong. But tonight the moon seemed an omen. Maybe she shouldn't go.

But there was something else. If she didn't go, she would always wonder what might have happened. Maybe it was better to follow Collin's philosophy. Why not try it? If you feel yourself falling, dive. No fear. Take it to the end. She'd go with Zahi.

She jumped off the bed, hurriedly pulled on sweats, then wrapped bright pink and purple boas around her neck. She was going to have fun. She was sick of all the baby games at Planet Bang and the La Brea High dances. This was going to be the big time.

As she spread glitter on her neck and face her spirits soared, but when she accidentally touched her moon amulet, a prayer tumbled from her lips, *"O Mater Luna, Regina nocis, adiuvo me nunc."*

She sat back on her bed. What was happening to her? That prayer only came out during times of great danger.

She looked behind her as if she expected to see someone standing in the corner of her room.

Then the doorbell rang.

CHAPTER THiRTEEN

ZAHI LEANED AGAINST the doorjamb. He looked sexy and handsome, dressed in khakis and a sweatshirt. His presence had a calming effect on her. "You look wonderful." He admired her.

She hurriedly locked and closed the door, then and followed him out to the car.

"You have the directions?" she asked.

He smiled and opened the car door. "On the seat." She picked up the directions, sat down, and snapped her seat belt into place.

They drove up the Antelope Valley Freeway at breakneck speed, then took the Pearblossom

Highway through a forest of spiny Joshua trees and cactus scrub. Moonlight illuminated the desert, giving it a strange underwater glow. She rolled down her window and the sweet smell of desert sage filled the car.

"Look." Zahi pointed to the blue and pink laser lights piercing the night sky. Latticework towers on the horizon looked like a strange spaceship.

"Cool," she breathed softly.

As they drove closer the traffic became more congested. Then it stopped. Guys wearing walkie-talkie headsets waved flashlights and directed kids to a parking area. Some impatiently drove off the road into deep sand and got stuck half on, half off the road, adding to the traffic jam.

The wind shrieked in and out of the car, but when it stopped, the music was loud enough to carry across the desert.

"Let's turn back and walk," Serena said with mounting excitement.

"You don't mind the walk?" Zahi asked.

"I'm too wound up. The walk will give me time to calm down."

He leaned over and kissed her. "No calming down tonight," he whispered, then he spun the car, gunned the motor, and left a track of rubber on the two-lane highway.

He found a place at the edge of the highway that looked good and parked. They got out and started walking. The desert wind blasted around them, thrashing their hair and slapping their clothes against their bodies. Her boa followed after her like a flying snake.

Soon they were walking with other kids dressed like techno hippies in bright neon colors, carrying light sticks and Day-Glo flowers. Throbbing brass and machinelike sounds drowned out the howling wind. They passed a girl selling T-shirts with the rave culture's neo-hippie motto, PLUR, written on the front and underneath, in small letters, PEACE, LOVE, UNDERSTANDING, RESPECT.

Kids sold water, glow sticks, flares, smiley faces, Day-Glo plastic jewelry, and pacifiers from their cars.

They had gone about a mile when they

stopped and Zahi gave their tickets to a man wearing a floppy purple hat.

Serena stepped into the mix. The huge size of the gathering made her feel as if she was going to the county fair. The music beat faster than machine-gun fire, hitting 160 beats a minute. The energy pulsed through her as rapidly as the beat.

She held her arms out and started twirling. Zahi grabbed her around the waist and they twirled wildly together until they were both out of breath.

He kissed her lightly and then they started walking again.

The vibrations grew stronger as they pushed toward the towering speakers. The sound quaked through her chest, rocking ribs, heart, and bone. It felt excitingly weird and good. She tried to soak in as much of the delicious energy as she could.

Some of the kids leaned against the speakers, bathing in the throbbing beat.

Zahi took her hand and they walked through another group of kids, who were sucking on plastic baby pacifiers while they danced.

"Why are they doing that?" Serena asked.

"The pacifiers ease the teeth-grinding effect from the Ecstasy," he explained. "Don't worry. We don't need drugs for thrills." He leaned down and kissed the side of her head. "We'll enjoy a greater energy. I promise."

Up on the stage a deejay wearing thick gold chains over a black T ran back and forth between four turntables. Everyone was into the dancing.

Serena snapped her light stick and started moving, the beat too fast to catch. She waved her arms and head.

"Wait," Zahi mouthed.

She didn't want to wait.

"Dance," she yelled over the music, and hopped over to him. He pressed his body next to hers, his hand curling tightly around her waist. She looked into his eyes, so dark and reflecting the moon's silver light. He almost looked supernatural, like a creature of the night. Why hadn't she noticed how compelling his eyes were before?

She felt his breath on her lips. The desert

wind rushed around them as if it were trying to separate them.

"Wait for what?" she asked even though she was sure he couldn't hear her. She didn't want an answer; she wanted his kiss. His lips were inches from hers now.

"Promise yourself to me?" he said.

A deep blush rose inside her.

"Maybe." She wanted love, respect, and trust first. She wasn't in a hurry. She glanced up at him and boldly put her arms around his neck. She did want a kiss.

He smiled and looked down at her, taking his time and making her hungry with anticipation. He looked darkly beautiful, his eyes lustrous. Then he pressed his lips on hers. A jolt of pleasure rushed through her body. His hands traced up her back.

"Let's go over there." He pointed to a smaller group of kids on the steep rocky slopes of a nearby butte. The jagged rocks and sheer sandstone outcroppings were silhouetted against the indigo sky. The kids danced around a fire in some antic neotribal way. It looked like fun.

"Okay." She closed her eyes and lifted her face for another kiss, but he was already pulling away.

They shoved through dancers waving Christmas tinsel, boas, flags, flowers, beads, and light sticks.

When they reached the fire, Serena climbed on a bolder and started dancing again.

She whooped, glad she had decided to come. Then from the corner of her eye she noticed something strange. One by one the kids around her had stopped dancing and were staring up at her.

Their eyes glowed phosphorescent.

She stood motionless.

Punkers. Pierced lips. In the fire's flickering light, their tattoos looked like the he-goat depicted on the devil card in her tarot deck.

She jumped off the bolder. Why would Followers be at a rave? Even these newer aggressive ones? They feared the full moon, when their eyes turned phosphorescent and ordinary people could feel their evil.

Their eyes flashed with anticipation.

She stood in front of Zahi, ready to protect him.

The fire raged upward when she did.

"We've got a problem," she said to Zahi, hoping he could hear her. "We have to leave now. I can't explain why. Just trust me."

Suddenly, she was doubtful that she could fight so many of them by herself.

She turned to push Zahi farther away. When she did, he smiled and lifted his left hand. A glossy impression of her moon amulet glimmered on his palm.

She now understood why the devil, the moon, and the high priestess had shown up in the spread. The cards had been trying to warn her. Even as she reproached herself for being so incredibly stupid, she knew there was still part of her that wanted Zahi.

"You would not be the first goddess to join the Atrox," he said. Or was he speaking inside her mind? His words felt seductive and compelling. "You're smarter than the other goddesses. Even Maggie sees it. She's been trying to tell you."

He touched her and she backed away from him.

"The dark of the moon was sacred to the witch goddess, Hekate," he said. "It could be sacred to you as well. All you have to do is step into the fire and become immortal. Why do you need the Daughters of the Moon when you can become even more powerful and have eternal life?"

The flames twisted, the tips radiating a strange whiteness that seemed almost pure. Sparks burst into the air and continued to glow as they twirled up and up.

"*Lecta,*" Zahi said softly.

The fire responded and flames shot toward them like searching arms eager to embrace her.

"*Lecta.*" Another Follower joined in, and soon they were all chanting, "*Lecta! Lecta!*"

She could no longer hear the music from the mammoth speakers, only the cold fire calling to her.

The blaze reached higher.

"Make me proud," Zahi coaxed. "Live with me for eternity."

The flames roared with impatience.

"I won't," she finally spoke. "I won't go in the fire."

"No matter." Zahi smiled malevolently. "I will take you to it."

He grabbed her wrists and began to pull her toward the flames. The dark anger made his face even more perfect than it had been before, a purely evil beauty.

She tried to fight him with mental force, but his power was stronger and her head pulsed with the rhythm of his thoughts. Her temples throbbed as the pain inside her head became unbearable. Her vision clouded as his power cut through hers like shards of broken glass.

 SERENA SAW the full moon through the wavering flames.

"*O Mater Luna, Regina nocis, adiuvo me nunc,*" she whispered, chanting the prayer like a mantra.

"The prayer will not help you, Serena." Zahi smirked.

She was close enough to the fire to feel its sweeping coldness.

She continued to look at the moon through the turbulent fire. Suddenly she knew Zahi couldn't harm her. Even alone she was protected. She gazed at the moon's brilliance, breathed deeply, and felt power surge through her.

Zahi noticed the change. "Do you think the moon will protect you?" he whispered across her mind. "Look again."

Darkness crept over the edge of the moon.

"The moon is entering the shadow of the earth," he said. "There is a full eclipse tonight. For two and a half hours you will be without the protection of your moon."

Serena looked up as the edge of night began to cross the moon.

Her power ebbed.

Zahi grabbed her hand.

It took all of her effort to block him from controlling her. And then he broke through her mental barrier with an explosive force. His thoughts flooded through her and took control again.

She looked at the flames licking the night sky and felt a lethargy take over.

She hesitated, then took one step forward and another.

"*Lecta*," the Followers began to chant again.

The flames radiated out and encircled her wrists with terrifying coldness. She shivered. The cold penetrated her bones as she stood at the edge of the fire.

Her tears turned to small ice crystals that slid down her cheeks. Then Zahi's mind wrapped completely around her like protective dark wings, and her resistance died.

CHAPTER FIFTEEN

POWERFUL HANDS GRABBED her shoulders and suddenly yanked her back. Zahi left her mind with a suddenness that caused a painful jolt. She fell to the ground. She shook her head, the hypnosis over, and inched back as glaring, angry flames howled skyward, then tracked along the coarse soil trying to grab her and pull her back.

Stanton stood protectively over her.

The power emanating from Stanton and Zahi made the air crackle as if great electrical currents were flowing between them. The small hairs on the back of her neck rose and the air became too thick to breathe. She didn't have the strength yet to stand.

The Followers loyal to Zahi crowded around him. They could not attack without his order.

Stanton stood alone. Was he powerful enough to fight off Zahi?

The air became heavy with the smell of ozone, and then the air exploded violently with a roll of thick thunder. Stillness followed. She didn't know who had won. She took a deep breath and then another.

Stanton ran to her and grabbed her hand.

"Come on!" he said. "We have to get away before Zahi recovers."

She glanced back. Zahi appeared to be frozen in a trance.

She didn't want to stay with Zahi and his Followers, but at the same time she didn't completely trust Stanton. Why had he rescued her?

"Haven't you figured out yet that I was telling you the truth?" he snapped angrily. "Of course not. You don't remember because Zahi hid those memories from you again."

She tried to stand but her legs were too shaky. Her head throbbed. Seeing that she couldn't run, Stanton swung her up in his arms and carried her.

"Up there." He motioned with his head. "We'll hide in the rocks."

He ran into the rocky terrain of the butte, carrying Serena. Night predators scrambled away as he wound in and out of the rocks and shadows. The laser lights and cold fire created strange shifting shadows across the face of the sandstone outcropping.

Stanton tripped over a rock. They fell and he tumbled on top of her.

"Sorry," he said. "Are you okay?"

"No." Pain racked her bones.

She suddenly realized he was still lying on top of her, his body warm against hers. And she wasn't repulsed, not at all. Her hands moved against her will, curling up around the hard muscles on his back. She looked into his blue eyes, visible in the dark, so startlingly honest.

"Stanton," she whispered, and as she said his

name a deluge of memories flooded over her, swirling with tumultuous speed around her every thought. He wasn't pushing them into her mind. The recollections were forcing their way back from some dark hidden place deep inside her.

He touched her cheek softly as if he knew what was happening. She closed her eyes.

"I'm sorry." She spoke with deep penetrating sadness as she finally recalled how many times Stanton had warned her about Zahi. "I should have believed you."

"How could you?" he asked. "He only left you with bad memories of me."

She lay quietly beneath him, immersed in the memories. How could she feel this way about someone who had dedicated his life to evil?

She could tell by the disappointment on his face that he read her bewilderment and alarm. She looked away.

"It takes longer for the emotions to return," he said simply, and then he motioned for her to be quiet.

A shadow fell over them.

She looked up. A Follower stood nearby. His spiky orange hair and the hoops pierced through eyebrows, lips, and nose made him look edgy and hard-core.

She made her mind blank so that if this Follower had learned how to sense thoughts he wouldn't be able to pick up hers.

The Follower shook his head, then rubbed his eyes, and she knew Stanton was working his mind. He fingered his nose ring, looked in the opposite direction, and ambled away from them.

Stanton got off her and helped her up, then they peered from behind the boulder.

The Followers swarmed through the jagged rocks.

"It's only moments before another one finds us," Stanton whispered. "We're going to have to split up."

"Okay." She nodded and looked up the bluff. It was a steep climb but the only way she saw to escape.

Stanton touched her cheek and turned her head to face him. "If you have the power to read minds and steal memories, then you also have the power to cloud minds."

"I've never done that before." She shrugged. "I don't know if I can."

"You'll have to use that part of your power to protect yourself in case one of them finds you."

"But I don't know how." Usually she would practice her new skills with the other Daughters before trying them on anyone alone.

"I'm going to distract them," Stanton said. "Hopefully, Zahi will chase after me. He'll think you're the easier prey and come back for you later."

"Thanks." She shot him an angry look.

He almost laughed. "I said he'd *think*. He doesn't know you the way I do. Sneak back to the rave and hide in the crowd."

She realized suddenly that he was going to sacrifice himself to save her. Maybe he could fight off Zahi, but what about all of the other Followers?

She touched his hand. "Two together have better odds."

"No." He shook his head. "I can explain

stealing you from Zahi because the Atrox thrives on competition among its Followers, but I wouldn't be able to explain helping you escape."

"The Regulators," she remembered with a sudden chill.

"The Atrox has to believe that I stole you from Zahi for my own prize and then you escaped from me."

"Be careful," she whispered and looked at the shadows. They seemed natural enough, but the Atrox was always around, sending shadows like tentacles as its eyes.

"Don't worry," Stanton assured her when he saw her studying the shadows. "It's not here."

"How can you tell?"

"Centuries of experience," he said with a grim laugh, then he stood.

"Caprimulgus!" he yelled angrily.

She translated his Latin. "Milker of goats?" It would have been funny if her hands hadn't been shaking so fiercely.

"Trust me. It's a big insult," Stanton explained.

"Let's run up the butte and find a better place to hide," she suggested, worried for his safety.

"No," he said firmly. "Our chances are better if we separate."

Serena peeked around the corner of the boulder as Stanton hollered, *"Caper!"*

The word made Zahi furious. She flinched in anticipation, but nothing happened. Apparently his power wasn't strong enough to confront Stanton from a distance, because she didn't feel a change in the air.

"Caper!" Stanton yelled again.

She'd have to ask Maggie what *caper* meant. Stanton read her mind.

"I just called him a he-goat. That's the way people with an ordinary knowledge of Latin would translate it, but I really called him the smell of an armpit." Stanton looked at her doubtful expression. "Maybe you have to have been around for a few hundred years to understand."

He bent down quickly and kissed the top of her head. "Good luck."

Stanton darted over the rocks. The Followers ran after him. Stones and pebbles rolled down the butte behind him.

When the running footsteps were too distant to hear, she stood and looked around the rock outcropping.

A Follower grabbed her. The girl was trying to look deadly dangerous with her black lipstick, piercings, and partially shaved head.

"Goddess," she whispered fiercely into Serena's ear, and bent her arm back painfully. "Zahi! I've got her."

CHAPTER SIXTEEN

THE FOLLOWER HELD Serena tightly, but her mind didn't try to control her. She started to yell again, but before she could, Serena pushed quickly into her mind.

The girl's mouth closed and a whimper died in her throat.

She had no barriers against Serena's entrance. Her mind was frightenly dark and empty, all hope surrendered to the Atrox, no dreams, no plans for the future, only a vast desert of days stringing hopelessly before her. She was only an initiate, waiting to see if the Atrox would accept her as a

Follower. Serena relaxed. Someone who had recently turned to the Atrox was the easiest to save. Serena didn't need to stay in her mind to control her. She slipped back out.

"You're new, aren't you?" Serena commented, clicking her tongue pierce against her teeth.

The girl frowned.

"They haven't even told you anything about mind control yet. Don't they trust you?"

The girl didn't seem to understand.

"Sorry," Serena said. "You're about to displease your master." She let the power build inside her head and then she released the force.

The girl put her hands over her face. She leaned against the rock, then slid down its side. Still holding her head, she spread her fingers and looked dumbly out at the shadows in front of her, her eyes uncomprehending.

"You'll thank me someday," Serena told her, wondering if the girl had parents who were frantically waiting at home to hear from her. "The Atrox isn't going to allow you in now that you've let me escape."

Rocks tumbled down the side of the butte.

Serena looked up. Several Followers were running toward her, jumping over craggy rocks. Zahi stood at the top, his hair whipping around his face. She could feel and see the strength of Zahi's mind crackling through the night air, sparking off rocks and boulders, searching for her.

She turned to run but tripped over a rock. She tumbled and looked back.

"Stop!" Zahi yelled. She slowed, but only for an instant.

She glanced up at the moon, almost lost in the earth's shadow now.

She ran crazily, leaping over cactus shrubs and rocks, until finally she was pushing through the twirling, jumping, spinning bodies.

And then she saw Morgan dancing with two boys.

"Morgan!" she shouted, even though she knew Morgan couldn't hear her over the beat of the music. She ran to her.

Morgan had braided her hair with Christmas tinsel and strapped fluffy angel wings on her back. She'd never looked so funked-out and cool. The guys dancing with her wore yellow, pink, and violet glow hoops around their necks and arms, reflector tape on their jeans, and large floppy hats.

"Morgan," Serena called again as she drew closer.

One of the guys tapped Morgan and pointed to Serena.

Morgan stopped dancing, her fists on her hips. "What do you do? Follow me around? The cool doesn't rub off, Serena."

"I need to talk to you." Serena pulled her away from the boys.

"Why don't you go back to geek heaven with all your bizarre friends," Morgan snapped and yanked her arm away from Serena.

"This is way serious," Serena insisted. "I need your help."

"Right." Morgan gave her a spiteful smile.

"Remember what happened to you a month back with those kids who hang out with Stanton?"

Morgan took a sudden step backward and gave her a petulant look. "You can't threaten me. I'm not afraid of you."

"Why would you be afraid of *me?*" Serena demanded. "It's the others—"

"Please," Morgan said, and pulled on a gold chain hanging around her neck. A charm that looked curiously like a standing he-goat dangled on the end of the chain. "Zahi gave me this charm. He said it could ward off the evil eye and protect me from your black magic."

The charm looked demonic and evil.

"I think the charm is bad luck." Serena felt suddenly worried for Morgan's safety.

"Right," Morgan smirked. "I figured you'd say something like that. Did I mess up your plans? I guess you can't cast any more spells on me. What did you want to do? Get me to stay away from Collin? Have me make a fool out of myself again? I'm so on to you. You may be able to fool the others into thinking you're just a regular kid who likes to study and dress weird, but I know the truth and I'm going to tell everyone."

Serena looked quickly around. How soon before the Followers found them? Morgan was vulnerable because she'd already had a run-in with them. Serena didn't feel as if she had enough power to fight them all. She grabbed Morgan's hand.

"We're in danger here. We have to leave."

"I'm only in danger from you and your magic."

Someone grabbed Serena from behind.

She let out a cry.

CHAPTER SEVENTEEN

S HE TURNED, ready to fight Zahi.

It was one of Morgan's dumb boyfriends.

"Witch, huh?" the guy said in a teasing way and hung an uninvited arm over her shoulder. The brim of his floppy hat hit Serena's head. "You want to put a spell on me?"

"Get off me," Serena said and tried to push him away.

"Voodoo me," he leered and tried to kiss her.

"Go back to Morgan." She shoved harder.

He stumbled backward, then smiled stupidly at Serena and started dancing in weird jerking steps.

Serena started to walk away from them when he grabbed her again.

"I said leave me alone!" She turned, ready to punch him, but looked into Zahi's smiling face instead.

"Goddess." His eyes dilated and glowed.

Then the night air shuddered and his energy burst into strands of light that twisted toward her. She understood his power to control her now, the subtle way he hid memories from her. Before he pushed into her mind, she sent all her force out and tunneled into his. Maybe she could cloud his thoughts and use that moment to escape. He wouldn't be expecting her attack.

She thrust into his mind and knew immediately she had made a dangerous mistake. She felt his laughing embrace as his power sucked her deeper and deeper inside him. The rave fell away and she stood in cold darkness. She began to shiver. Something menacing hovered in the shadows around her.

The Atrox. The black night shadows snaked around her, caressing her with unmistakable tenderness and coaxing her forward. What did it want her to see? She took one slow step and then another, afraid of what she might see when the shadows cleared.

"Look, my chosen one," a steely voice commanded.

The shadows cleared and a mirror stood before her. She looked at her reflection. She was different, her green eyes as deep as newly cut emeralds, her skin flawless and glowing with a strange light. A shiver traveled through her as she felt her evil potential. She had an impulse to run, but where? She was trapped inside Zahi's mind.

"Look," the shadow whispered and cradled her. "Look at what I offer you."

She stared in the mirror again and her reflection changed. She held her cello, lovingly embraced between her knees, hand delicately pulling the bow across the strings. The picture was mesmerizing.

"Look deeper," the voice challenged.

She touched the gilt edges of the mirror, and suddenly she had no desire to flee. She was playing on a stage, a symphony behind her, the audience enraptured.

"You shall have that." The voice spoke with complete confidence.

How had the Atrox known her most secret dream? The dream she had been afraid to voice even to her best friend Jimena.

The music rolled over her in waves, her fingers so sure on the strings. Tears formed in the sides of her eyes. Yes, this was what she wanted more than anything, but she had been afraid she wouldn't . . . couldn't have the time to make it come true. And here it was. Success without the sacrifice. She would do anything—

Someone tackled her to the ground. The mirror shattered around her, bursting into vapor. Her chin hit the dirt and sharp pain spun inside her head.

CHAPTER EIGHTEEN

THE FALL RELEASED HER from Zahi's hold. Her head ached and thin lines wavered in front of her eyes as if Zahi were still trying to pull her back into his world of dark promise. She looked up.

Zahi stood over her and seemed as baffled as she felt.

She looked around, unable to grasp what had happened. Kids danced wildly, their feet stomping near her. The rapid pulse of the music beat through her.

"Jimena?!"

"Did you think I was going to punk out on you?" Jimena said, and helped her stand.

"Thanks." She took Jimena's hand and stood.

Zahi's eyes burned yellow, his power sweeping around them, but he didn't seem as invincible as before.

Jimena and Serena concentrated on pushing back his mental attack. Serena felt lost in her own power as it filled the air with an invisible force. Their moon amulets gleamed white and then shot blinding purple bits of fire into the air. Kids nearby stopped dancing and waved their hands through the air in amazement. Some jumped and tried to catch the purple embers floating in the wind like thick snowflakes.

Serena and Jimena released their power.

Zahi stumbled back.

"Come on," Jimena said, and grabbed Serena's hand. "You've done enough fighting for tonight."

Serena turned and bumped into Morgan.

Morgan screamed and jumped back. She

held out her he-goat charm pinched between white trembling fingers and pointed it at Serena as if it were a knife.

"Stay back," she yelled.

"Did Zahi do something to her?" Serena asked Jimena as they started pushing through the crowd.

"You were in a trance or something when Zahi had you," Jimena explained. "Then she saw what we did to Zahi. She's probably afraid you're going to put another spell on her."

"Another? I never put a first one on her."

"Don't waste energy trying to figure out Morgan, we've got to get away from here before Zahi and his band of Followers get after us."

Serena watched Zahi put his arm around Morgan. Morgan looked up at him with a coy smile and stared into his eyes.

"We've got to get Morgan." She started back and Jimena stopped her.

"Look again," Jimena warned.

Morgan lost the fast beat of the music. She entwined her arms around Zahi, still lost in his eyes. Her hips moved snakelike to music only she could hear. Zahi placed his hands on her waist and glanced back at Serena.

"Mine now," he mouthed, or maybe he had brushed the words across her mind, because she heard them clearly.

Serena darted back to fight Zahi.

Jimena grabbed her hard. "*No seas tonta.* You did what you could. He only took Morgan to get at you. You think you can fight him now?"

Zahi's punk Followers swarmed around him and glared at her.

She could feel Zahi's taunting laughter as she finally turned and followed Jimena.

They continued pushing through the dancers until they were running past the buzzing generators. The fumes from the generators drifted away, replaced by the aroma of desert sage. They slowed and started trekking across the desert through the spiked and twisted Joshua trees. The lunar eclipse threw an eerie reddish color across the moon's face.

Serena spoke first. "How did you know where to find me?"

"Over at your house, when I touched your forehead to see if you had a fever, I got a premonition so big it almost knocked me on my butt. I saw you at the rave with Zahi. Didn't take much figuring to know what had caused your flu."

"I'm sorry." Serena looked down. "But how did you know I needed help?"

"Because you'd never put some *vato* in front of your friends. And for sure you would never lie to me. So I got to thinking about what you'd said about Stanton."

"His warning to me about Zahi?"

"Yeah. Plus Zahi transferred to our school about the same time the new Followers showed up. That's when I knew he'd put a hold on you. So I blasted up to the desert like a rocket. I would have been there sooner but I had to park about a mile out."

"Thanks," Serena said, and hugged Jimena.

They came to a dirt road.

"Let's take this." Jimena pointed. "It should hook up to the highway."

Their feet crunched over gravel and dirt.

Without Joshua trees and scrub to shelter them, the wind battered against them in unrelenting whirls, driving dust into their eyes.

"I saw the Atrox," Serena said slowly. "At least I think I did. It wasn't so scary."

"Wasn't?" A look of surprise held Jimena's face.

Serena shook her head. "Do you ever wonder why we're doing this? I mean, we've got Followers always chasing us down and it makes a real mess of our social life. What happens if we tell Maggie we don't want to do it anymore?"

"We can't. It's our destiny. You know that." Jimena sounded concerned. "Besides, I figure there's something important waiting for us."

"But Maggie can't even tell us what's waiting for us. She should tell us what happens when we turn seventeen," Serena complained.

"Maybe she doesn't know," Jimena suggested.

"She knows," Serena said with sudden anger. "Maybe going with the Atrox is easier."

Jimena stopped and grabbed Serena's elbow. "You *loca*? What's got you?"

Did she dare tell her the truth? "I mean, why not become queen of the dark?"

"Because," Jimena insisted.

"That's not an answer. Why be good when we're in so much danger and we don't even know if we get a future? If the Atrox can give us so much, why not be bad?"

"I know bad." Jimena spoke quietly. "It's not the answer." She fingered the scars on her arm as if the return to her memories were making them throb. She caught Serena looking at her. "If you don't have the scars, then you didn't have the life."

Jimena was silent for a long time, the desert wind lashing her hair into her eyes. "I didn't go looking for trouble at first, but it was always there. I felt like I was caught in this hole and I kept digging, thinking I could get out, but the hole just kept getting deeper and bigger. Then one night at a party, this guy walks in and he takes an AK-47 from his coat and starts shooting. I mean, *damn,* I'd never seen so many people die. He killed two of my home girls. So the next day at school I got a gun. I walked over to him, sitting all alone in his car and I shot him. I kept pulling the trigger till his friends stopped me. That was the first time I got sent to camp."

"Did he die?"

"Lucky for me he didn't. His car got most of the bullets. But I was still going to kill him as soon as I got out."

"Did you?" Serena asked softly. Jimena had never told her this much about her life before. She had thought Jimena had gone to camp for stealing cars.

"I got out and that's when I turned evil," she continued. "I must have been evil to do the things I did before I got caught up again. I didn't care. I was jacking cars and taking all kinds of risks. Some days I even scared myself. But I couldn't stop. I didn't want to. Being bad and breaking all the rules can make you feel invincible. There's power in that . . . for a while . . . and then . . ."

"What?"

"There must be something deep inside people that doesn't like to be bad, because afterward I felt like I was all alone in the world and nobody could love me after the things I'd done. But I didn't want to give up the feeling of power I had when I was bad. I felt above everyone. Bigger. Better. A real hard-rock gangster."

They walked down the road in silence, listening to the haunting wind.

"I got caught again, went to camp—but this time—"

"That was right before I met you," Serena added.

Jimena nodded. "But this time something snapped and I lost my anger. I mean I got in there and I was waiting in the holding tank with these shackles around my arms and waist and ankles, staring at the gray wall and I thought, I do not want to spend my life this way."

"But how did you get community service?"

"That was after I got out of camp. My home girls did the throw-down. They took this old woman's purse, but the cops caught me. The cops wanted me to talk, but no way was I going to be a rat-head. The judge saw something different in my eyes this time. I could see it on her face, the way she smiled at me like she knew I'd finally learned my lesson. She knew I'd changed. I had. Used to be I wouldn't have even talked to someone like you, who followed the rules. I thought I was better because I didn't have to. Now we're kicking it like we've known each other forever."

Serena put her arm around Jimena.

"So maybe it looks good, what the Atrox showed you," Jimena continued. "But after, when you're alone, it won't look so good—won't feel good, either. It's worth nothing, 'cause that's what you end up with."

They reached the crossroads and stopped. A small house was nestled under a row of swaying cypress trees. Flames flapped furiously from four rusted oil drums in the front yard, making shadows jig and twist around the trees and house.

"Who'd live all the way out here?" Serena wondered.

"Doesn't matter," Jimena said. "Let's cut across the yard."

They stepped into the yard and a shadow

moved in the darkness under the cypress tree, then another stalked forward.

"What was that?" Serena asked nervously.

"Your imagination is in high gear." Jimena laughed.

Then three large black dogs charged from the shadows, teeth bared, ears back. Their paws and nails scattered dirt, pebbles, and desert dust.

"*Ay!*" Jimena yelled, and jumped behind Serena.

"Here, nice doggy," Serena crooned in a soothing voice, but the sound of her words only seemed to make the dogs angrier. Their snarls grew louder.

The first dog pounced as an old woman wrapped in a black shawl stepped out onto the small wood porch. The wind caught the tail of her shawl and whipped it up and around, tangling it in her long white hair.

Serena could feel the dog's hot breath on her face. She stiffened, too stunned to run, and waited for the teeth to bite into her cheek.

The old woman whistled.

The dog whimpered and turned back, its paws pushing off Serena's chest.

The other two dogs slid in the loose gravel, turning. Then all three ran back to the woman, who now stood in the yard in front of the porch.

Serena wiped the hot spittle from her cheek, then rubbed her hand on her sweats.

"Man, I can fight an ancient evil," Jimena muttered. "But give me a good ol' American dog and I turn to yellow Jell-O."

"I'm right there with you." Serena didn't need to turn around to know that Jimena was trembling as badly as she was.

The dogs pranced around the woman, licking her hand. The one that had attacked Serena now lay on his back in the dirt yard, begging for a belly scratch.

"Who is that woman?" Jimena whispered.

"I don't know."

"Let's get out of here. The crossroads are *peligroso*. They're dangerous, eh?"

But neither of them moved. There was something about the woman that held them. She wore three iron keys on a chain around her neck, and when she turned toward them the keys hit each other with a soft clanking sound.

"Who says the crossroads are dangerous, anyway?" Serena asked, unable to take her eyes off the unusual woman.

"My *abuelita*."

"Girls," the woman called.

And they both jumped.

"Come here, please." Her voice seemed remarkably young and strong.

"Yeah, what?" Jimena shouted. "You got something to say, we can hear you from here."

Serena elbowed her. "She probably wants to apologize for letting her dogs scare us."

"She's a witch, a ghost, or *la llorona*," Jimena said.

"How can you tell?"

"You got eyes."

"She's okay." Serena grabbed Jimena's elbow and pulled her forward. "She's just someone's grandmother living out here."

"Check her out."

"All right." Serena pushed gently into the woman's mind. She couldn't. There was nothing there. Impossible.

"You picking up anything?" Jimena asked impatiently.

"No." Serena shrugged. "I think I used up all my energy tonight. How 'bout you?"

"Yeah, but I don't need a premonition. It's common sense. Strange old woman. Living alone. I don't want to go inside and see all the dead rats and cats and kids in her refrigerator and watch her sing over the bones."

The woman started walking toward them. Her milky brown eyes were deep-set and filled with knowledge. "I've been expecting you," she said.

"That's it." Jimena threw up her hands. "I'm outta here."

Serena grabbed her arm and made her stay.

"Have you young women ever heard of Hekate?" the woman asked, and petted the dogs prancing around her skirt.

"What about it?" Jimena said.

"Why are you asking us about Hekate?" Serena didn't believe in coincidences.

"She protected people from going the wrong way at the crossroads," the woman began.

"We're not going the wrong way, *viejecita*." Jimena crossed her arms. "My car's parked right over there."

"You'd be surprised." The woman's wrinkled lips turned up in another smile. Her crooked finger pointed in the opposite direction.

"Come on, Serena." Jimena started walking.

"I'm going to stay," Serena decided. She had a strange feeling this woman wanted to help her. "Get the car and come back for me."

"*¿Estás loca?*" Jimena was exasperated. "Haven't you had enough for one night?" She kicked the ground. The dogs growled and she stepped back.

"I need to talk to her."

"Whatever." Jimena shook her head and walked off.

Serena followed the woman inside. The dogs rushed around her and settled under a table in the middle of the room. The woman shut the door against a dust devil forming in the yard. The door rattled as the wind continued to rage.

Dozens of candles of differing shapes and colors lit the interior and cast a warm glow about the room. The air smelled of vanilla and pinecones.

The old woman sat down at the oak table in the middle of the room. Two plates, two cups, a dish of petits fours, and a teapot sat on the table as if she had been expecting company.

"Come in and sit down," the old woman offered.

Serena sat across from her. One of the dogs rested its head on her shoe, its nose cold against her ankle.

The woman poured two cups of tea, and in the candlelight her face looked sad.

"Did your electricity go out?" Serena asked, but she already knew the answer.

"No, I prefer the dark. You could say the dark is sacred to me."

"Why?"

"Because everyone must travel through the dark in order to reach the light. I suppose that means they must all come to me eventually for advice."

"You are Hekate?" Serena whispered.

"Hekate." The woman repeated the name as if the feel of the word on her tongue awakened something inside her. "No." She picked up the plate of petits fours.

"Are you lonely living all the way out here?"

"Some of us must bear more in life than others," the woman answered softly.

Serena braced herself to hear the woman bemoan her solitude.

"But that can be a blessing." She offered Serena the petits fours.

Serena took one and bit in.

"Some people want an easy life, they want the fame and fortune and none of the struggle." She stopped and looked at Serena. "I suppose you have a dream?"

"Yes," Serena answered as the wind shrieked

over the roof and pounded against the door, demanding entrance.

"I can see what you want and yet it's frightening to you, wondering if you can work hard enough to achieve it."

Serena nodded.

The wind screamed again under the door. The candles flickered and underneath the table the dogs whimpered.

"I love the wind," the woman said, looking behind her. "All women have the power of the wind inside them, deep in their souls. The problem is . . ."

Her eyes looked at the ceiling as the wind skated across the roof, lifting shingles. She smiled and turned back to Serena.

"The problem is most women let this force die out to a breeze when a whirlwind is needed. When her forces are gathered and focused, she can do anything. It's when the force is scattered that she fails."

The house shook and then the wind broke open the door, whirled around the room, and blew out the candles. Then it left as suddenly as it had come, leaving only the dark and the smell of candle smoke in the room.

"You see," the woman said, and reached under the table to pet her whining dogs. "It can be quite powerful when focused."

The roar of mufflers sounded outside. Then Jimena walked across the porch. The boards creaked under her feet. She peeked inside. "Serena?"

"Yeah?" Serena didn't move.

"Let's roll," Jimena said impatiently.

"Thank you." Serena stood and walked to the door.

The wind had become no more than a whisper now. The flames in the oil drums licked lazily toward the night sky and reflected off the blue fender of Jimena's car.

The woman followed them to the door, the dogs by her side. Before she closed the door, she spoke to Serena in Latin. *"Id quod factum est, infectum esse potest."*

"What do you mean?" Serena asked.

"Use it," the woman said, and lifted a chain holding one of the keys from around her neck and placed it around Serena's neck.

"What is the key to?" Serena examined it in the dim light.

"You'll know if you ever need it." The woman smiled, went back inside, and closed the door.

On the drive back to L.A., Jimena asked, "What did she say to you, anyway?"

"Id quod factum est, infectum esse potest."

Jimena thought for a moment. "What has been done can be undone. What does that mean?"

"I'm not sure," Serena said, and fingered the key. Then she thought about Zahi, and suddenly she knew what she had to do.

CHAPTER NINETEEN

THE NEXT DAY, Serena called Zahi and asked him to meet her near the Beverly Center.

The Sunday morning traffic was light, the air still, and a thin layer of gray clouds hung in the sky. Zahi walked up San Vicente, where she waited under the green awning of the Hard Rock Cafe.

"I changed my mind," she said when he reached her.

He placed his arm around her and whispered, his breath warm against her ear, "I knew you would." Then he leaned back and looked at her, his eyes filled with cruel delight and satisfaction. "Say it," he commanded.

She stared straight at him. "I'll step into the fire and become the witch goddess."

The wind whipped around them, spinning dirt, paper, and dried leaves from the gutter as if the Atrox had been listening and her promise had swept it into ecstasy. But then she caught the surprised look in Zahi's eyes and wondered if the whirlwind had come from a force inside her.

"Lecta," Zahi uttered with a slight tremor in his voice. "I will pick you up tonight. The moon rises at seven. I will be parked in your driveway at six-thirty."

"All right," she said, and walked away. He watched her as she stepped around the corner and walked past Todai and Ubon. She continued down the street to Jan's coffee shop.

Catty, Vanessa, and Jimena were waiting for her at a large booth in the back. It was warm and crowded inside and smelled of bacon, coffee, and fresh-squeezed orange juice. She slid into the booth. They had already ordered a Belgium waffle and a cup of coffee for her.

"You did it?" Jimena said.

Serena nodded.

"Did he say where you were going?" Vanessa asked and poured syrup over her waffle.

"No." Serena took a sip of hot coffee, hoping it would ease the chill inside her.

"It's dangerous." Jimena looked worried.

"It's the only thing that can be done," Serena declared. "We have to get rid of these new Followers. Zahi is their leader, and without him they'll be weakened."

"I'll go invisible and follow you," Vanessa suggested. "And then I'll come back and tell Catty and Jimena where you are."

"Hopefully, I'll get a premonition before then." Jimena took a deep breath. "We won't leave you hanging."

"If worse comes to worst," Catty added, "I'll take us back in time and then we'll just keep doing it until we get it right."

They all smiled, reassured, but Serena knew

it wouldn't work that way. They'd only have one chance. They seemed to understand.

"How are you going to fool Zahi?" Jimena asked.

"Yeah," Catty wondered. "What if he reads your mind and knows you're trying to trap him?"

"We should go talk to Maggie," Vanessa said. "She only lives a few blocks away."

"No." Serena didn't fully understand why she needed to do this without Maggie. "It's too late. I've made up my mind. Besides part of our mission is to find a way to release the Followers from their bondage to the Atrox."

"Yeah, but I don't think we're supposed to die trying," Catty pointed out. "Maggie's always helped us in the past."

"I agree." Vanessa pushed her food away. "It could be way too dangerous."

Serena looked at Jimena.

"I'm down for you." Jimena sighed. "But they're right. It's dangerous and I had that premonition of you standing in the cold fire."

"Look, you guys, you're either going to help

me or I'm going to do it by myself." Serena looked around the table. They each nodded their agreement.

That night Serena dressed to meet Zahi. She used a metallic green eye shadow on the top lids and the outer half of the bottom lids so that her eyes looked like a jungle cat's. Two coats of black mascara completed them, and then she smudged a light gold gloss on her lips.

She took a red skirt from the closet. The material was snakelike, shimmering black, then red. She slipped it on and tied the black strings of a matching bib halter around her neck and waist. She painted red-and-black glittering flames on her legs and rubbed glossy shine on her arms and chest.

Finally, she took the necklace she had bought at the garage sale and fixed it in her hairline like the headache bands worn by flappers back in the 1920s. The jewels hung on her forehead, making her look like an exotic maharani.

She sat at her dressing table and painted her

toenails and fingernails gold, then looked in the mirror. A thrill jolted through her as it always did. No matter how many times she saw her reflection after the transformation, her image always astonished her. She looked supernatural, a spectral creature, green eyes large, skin glowing, eyelashes longer, thicker. Everything about her was more forceful and elegant—an enchantress goddess. She couldn't pull away from her reflection. It was as if the warrior in her had claimed the night.

At last she took her moon amulet and placed it around her neck.

The doorbell rang. She grabbed the iron key and her high-heeled sandals, and hurried down the dark hallway, a faint rainbow light shimmering around her. Already she could feel Zahi's presence on the other side of the front door, his evil waiting to embrace her.

"Let him wait," she said softly to herself. She sat on the steps and slipped into her sandals. The ritual was complete now. She was ready for battle.

She stared down at the key in her hand. "Ready?" she whispered to Vanessa, who had been waiting invisible by the door. Then she slipped the key into her skirt pocket. She opened the door, waited for Vanessa to breeze past her, and stepped outside.

Zahi leaned against his car parked in the driveway, his legs crossed in front of him. When he looked up and saw her he gave an involuntary start and then a slow smile spread across his face. His deep brown eyes met hers and she saw the desire in them. She strolled over to him.

"I'm glad you changed your mind." He took her hand, turned it over, and kissed the palm. "Goddess," he whispered, and continued to hold her hand near his face, his breath warm on her skin.

She slowly pulled her hand away and worked hard to keep her mind blank. She could feel him softly treading through her thoughts.

He opened the car door. She climbed in and purposefully stretched her legs. Her dress rode up her thighs. She watched him watching her and didn't stop the stretch until she felt a chill brush across her back. Then she knew Vanessa was in the car.

"I'm settled in now," she announced coyly.

"Temptress," he said, smiling wickedly.

She took deep breaths as he hurried around the car and got in the driver's seat.

He turned the key in the ignition and the engine thundered. He backed the car from the drive with a squeal of brakes and headed toward Fairfax.

She let her head rest on the back of the car seat and smiled when she caught him casting sideways glances at her. Headlights, streetlights, and neon signs flashed light and shadow across the inside of the car.

"Your mind seems empty tonight," he said. His warm hand touched her knee, the fingers soothing.

"Oh," she started. "I—"

"You don't need to feel so nervous," he reassured her. The hand glided up her thigh.

"What happens after I become a Follower?" A flash of movement made her look in the back. Vanessa was crouched behind the driver's seat, slowly becoming visible. Her fear and nervousness were making her reappear.

"What?" Zahi's hand flew back to the steering wheel and he glanced at Serena suspiciously.

"I'll miss my friends," she said too loudly, trying hard to distract him and at the same time keep her mind empty.

"You will make new ones." He dismissed her worry and looked in the back. "What are you looking at?"

"Nothing," she whispered and ventured a glimpse into the back. Vanessa was invisible again. She breathed deeply and tried to relax.

They drove to the corner of Wilshire and Curson and parked near the Page Museum, where the La Brea tar pits were.

"Here?" she asked.

"Here." He got out of the car and then walked around the car, opened her door, and pulled her out.

He started to slam the door. She caught it.

He looked at her strangely.

"I felt dizzy for a moment," she said and

hoped he couldn't see the lie in her words. He had almost slammed the door on Vanessa.

"It will be over soon." His gleaming yellow eyes weren't even trying to hide his bold scrutiny of her body. "And then you will be mine for eternity."

Her heart beat more rapidly.

She felt a ruffle of air and knew Vanessa was out of the car. She slammed the car door. "Let's go."

They walked around the oozing tar pit, past the statues of the mammoths edging down to the water to drink.

As they continued around the Page Museum, blue and orange flames exploded into the night sky and sparkling red embers showered down on them like falling snow. An amber glow covered the park and the back of the L.A. County Art Museum.

She felt a light wind whisper through her hair and knew Vanessa was leaving to get Jimena and Catty.

They walked closer to the flames.

Zahi's Followers turned and smiled at her in welcome, their eyes yellow and needy. She thought she saw Morgan in the crowd, but the girl ducked behind two guys.

The fire seemed hungrily aware of her presence. Its cold flames shot out and curled around her, making her shiver. Patches of frost remained on her skin where the flames had caressed her.

"Step in," Zahi ordered.

She needed to wait until the other Daughters returned before she entered the fire. Otherwise her plan wouldn't work.

"Don't we party first?" She did her best to smile beguilingly at the other Followers, who seemed eager to do something more than look at flames.

Too late, she realized she had let her guard down. Zahi was in her mind, and now he understood her need to stall for time. Angrily, he tore the silver amulet from her neck, tossed it to the ground, and pushed her backward. She tripped and fell into the fire.

The flames shot up, and with a sudden roar,

sucked her into the middle of the fire.

She tried to breathe, but the bitter air felt too cold. Dancing flames surrounded her, and every time she turned to flee, more flames shot up until she was lost in the freezing inferno. Her bones began to ache from the cold. Her fingers grew numb. Frost gathered on her skin in crystalline snowflake patterns that glittered gold, then red. Her body throbbed, but just as the pain became unbearable, something sweet and longed-for penetrated her being. She gasped. Then with delight, she smoothed her hands down her body, over breasts, waist, hips, and thighs. The desire filled her, a wicked longing.

"*Lecta,*" Zahi breathed, and the ceremony began.

CHAPTER TWENTY

SERENA STRUGGLED AGAINST the caressing flames, the fierce hunger working inside her. Then the crackle of the flames grew still and cello music played, filling her mind with sweet promise. She stopped fighting. The flames soothed her and gave her a sensation of power. Her worries burned away as her strength grew.

Through the veil of flames, Zahi smiled triumphantly.

Abruptly, she reached through the shroud of fire and grabbed his arm.

He hadn't been able to read her intentions

because the Atrox had filled her mind with music. A look of total surprise and soul-wrenching fear covered his face as she yanked him into the flames.

The fire howled in anger and exploded into a blinding flash. The center of the blaze became piercingly cold. Sparks cascaded onto the lawn and trees, setting new fires.

Serena held Zahi tightly against her. *"Id quod factum est, infectum esse potest."*

"No!" Zahi screamed.

As she repeated the words, the fire became a swirling vortex, its shrieking colors circling with ever-increasing speed.

"What has been done can be undone!" Serena continued to repeat the words as the flames lashed at her with stinging cold.

In the distance the sirens of fire engines filled the night.

Serena looked through the violently rotating flames and saw Vanessa, Jimena, and Catty running toward her. They looked like goddesses; Vanessa dressed in shimmering blue, Jimena in lightning-strike silver, and Catty in wild strawberry pink, their hair bouncing in silky soft swirls with each step.

A police car with its light bar flashing electric blue drove into the park. The siren wound down and the officers jumped from the car. Some of the Followers ran. Morgan was one of them.

Serena grabbed Zahi's left hand and looked at the palm. The glimmering tattoo from her moon amulet had vanished. Zahi was mortal again. Serena pushed him from the fire.

He stumbled out and Jimena grabbed him. His remaining Followers circled him with anxious looks. Then one by one they began to scatter and run.

The first fire engine arrived and parked, followed quickly by a second and a third.

Firemen in yellow soot-covered protective clothing with fluorescent strips and domed helmets jumped from the trucks and began pulling hoses toward the fire as others worked with wrenches to attach the hoses to the hydrants.

Serena started to step from the flames, but the fire held her with almost human hands, inviting her to stay. The show of color and sparks became spellbinding and Serena could feel her sense of herself slipping away, pulled down into an ice-cold abyss. She ceased to resist. She breathed the flames. Its cold reached into her lungs, curled inside her chest and lay there like ice-blue flowers.

Jimena, Vanessa, and Catty watched in horror, their moon amulets glowing.

Serena stepped from the flames and stretched her arms over her head, enjoying the luxurious feel of her body. What would it be like to live forever? To see the next millennium, and the next? She opened her eyes and knew by the shock she saw in Jimena's eyes that her own now glowed phosphorescent.

She remembered the promise the Atrox had made to her, but she had no interest in the cello now and wondered why she would ever waste her time on something so foolish.

The fleeing Followers hesitated as if they sensed her growing power. A few jumped over the fire hoses and ran back to her.

She picked up her amulet where Zahi had tossed it. It seared her flesh. She glanced down. The outline of the moon was burned into her skin. She dropped it and Catty picked it up.

She watched the confusion on the faces of her friends as the power of the Atrox continued to grow inside her. She cherished the anguish she saw.

"Goddesses," she sneered, and then whooped exuberantly and prepared to fight her once best friends.

CHAPTER TWENTY-ONE

THE GLOW OF THE FIRE flickered nervously over the faces of Catty, Vanessa, and
Jimena. The fear in their eyes mirrored the change
they now saw in hers. Even Zahi, sprawled on the
grass, looked afraid of her.

Serena smiled contemptuously. She gave
them a little mental shove to demonstrate her new
power.

Vanessa took a step backward, shocked, but
Catty didn't flinch. "I'm not impressed," she said.

Jimena had a different look, one she couldn't

quite read. "We've got to get Serena back into the fire, quick before the firemen drag their hoses over here and put it out."

"Why?" Vanessa asked with growing worry.

Jimena kept her eyes on Serena while she spoke to Vanessa. "So we can burn the immortality off her. You don't get immortality without one big commitment to the Atrox." She took a resolute step forward.

Serena laughed at the determination she saw on Jimena's face.

"I don't think she's going to go." Vanessa seemed apprehensive.

"We'll make her," Catty replied.

Serena taunted Jimena. "You still think you're the tough goddess?"

Jimena didn't answer.

Serena laughed and gave them another mental jab, but this time Jimena had prepared for it and it didn't penetrate.

"So we're battling now," Serena said with glee.

Catty joined Jimena.

Vanessa stopped them. "Serena is a *Lecta*, a chosen one."

"So what?" Jimena tossed her head impertinently.

"Serena was invited into the fire," Vanessa explained. "Maggie said if you're not invited into the fire, the flames cause a horrible death. If the fire touches either of you—any of us—"

There wasn't the slightest hesitation on Jimena's face. "I'm not afraid of her," Jimena said. "She's just a chump with an attitude and she's going back in the fire." With even more resolve, she strutted forward.

Serena hesitated for the slightest second, wondering what it was inside Jimena that made her willing to risk an excruciating death to save Serena. And then she let the power build inside her until the air rippled.

Jimena suddenly lunged through the thick air and grabbed Serena's arm.

Serena let the force gather inside her mind, then she shoved it out at Jimena—one sharp invisible bolt of pure energy. Pain registered on

Jimena's face, but she didn't drop her hold.

Then Catty broke through the waving air and took her other arm.

"No!" Serena yelled, and the scream scraped up her throat with wretched pain, the sound so deep and angry it frightened her. It wasn't her voice.

Catty and Jimena pulled her toward the flames.

A fireman stopped them, his face in shadows cast from his helmet. "What the hell are you girls doing here?" he asked from behind his fire shield.

They ignored him and continued to pull Serena toward the flames.

"Get back," he yelled and plunged ahead, dragging the hose. When he was only ten feet from the blaze, he lifted his fire shield, then stripped a glove from one hand and waved it in the air. A look of awe covered his face.

"Cold," he said. "It's cold!"

Before he could say more, two other firefighters ran up behind him and took their positions on the hose. Water charged through the hose with sudden force and shot into the flames.

The fire consumed the water, hissing violently, and grew into a billowing tower.

"We've got to act now." Jimena reached for Serena again.

A policeman pushed them away from the shooting flames into the crowd that had gathered behind a barricade. Overhead a helicopter shot a column of light over the chaos. News vans set up their antennae and newscasters spoke rapidly into microphones.

"Firefighters have changed their approach," the newscaster spoke into a microphone as kids behind her threw gang signs and waved at the camera's eye. She continued, "At first fire officials thought the fire was set by an extreme group of punkers. Now they have determined it is a crude-oil fire, possibly caused by a methane gas explosion or seepage from the adjacent tar pits. They are now spraying a synthetic film-forming foam over the fire and do not anticipate any danger to the County Art Museum or the Page Museum."

The camera turned to the firefighters covering the flames with foam. The flames dwindled. Smoke billowed gently into the air, gliding in and out of the bars of white-blue light cast from the police and television helicopters overhead.

Serena brushed her hands through her hair, then turned and looked at the Followers who had gathered around her. "You're going to have to do better than you did tonight," she scolded with a brazen smile. Then her eyes caught Zahi, standing next to Jimena. Was he trembling? She hissed at him. He backed away.

"I was worried about kissing you." She laughed in disgust.

Her Followers laughed and the sound filled the night air with a chill.

"Goddesses," she said. "Not tonight but soon—I'll have the pleasure of destroying you."

She started walking saucily away, and enjoyed the looks she saw in the faces of the men, old and young.

Then she turned back. "Be sure to tell Maggie thanks for all the extra time she spent training me to use my gift. I'm sure it will come in handy."

Serena smiled maliciously and walked away.

CHAPTER TWENTY-TWO

*S*ERENA HADN'T GONE FAR when something made her skin prickle. She turned as Vanessa ran in front of the TV camera and dissolved into a ghostly shimmer.

What was she doing? Vanessa's greatest fear had always been that someone might see her become invisible, and now she was flaunting it. Why? Vanessa danced away from the TV camera, billowed on a breeze to the firefighters, and then like a circus performer, she fluttered in and out of focus.

The firefighters stopped spraying foam. The

first one took an involuntary step backward and knocked into the one behind him.

Newscasters and camera operators ignored the police officers. They pushed through the barricade and ran to the fire to capture the impossible on tape. Pandemonium broke loose. Vanessa led the crowd farther and farther away from the dwindling flames.

During the confusion, someone tackled Serena to the ground. Jimena!

Before she could push her away, Catty slipped the moon amulet around Serena's neck. Serena tried to yank it off, but Catty held her hands. The silver moon burned into Serena's skin and the searing pain distracted her. She couldn't concentrate enough to use her power. Jimena and Catty pulled her into the few smoldering flames while the crowd watched Vanessa do her invisibility dance.

The flames seethed and hissed and tried to push Serena from the fire. But Jimena stepped into the blaze, clasped Serena tightly, and made her stay.

"*Id quod factum est, infectum esse potest,*" Jimena

repeated, her voice becoming weaker and weaker.

The fire shrieked its protest. Cold spasms shuddered through Serena as the blaze began to burn away her immortality. Slowly, she returned from the wintry abyss into which she had been pushed. She saw a future again, not an endless string of days. Time seemed suddenly more precious, the night more beautiful. As the fire continued to consume her immortality, her allegiance to the Atrox retreated and her moon amulet no longer blistered her skin. Then she looked down and became aware of Jimena in the fire with her, writhing in excruciating pain.

"No!" she screamed.

She tried to step from the cold fire, but the blaze raged and refused to release her. The flames, like icy tendrils, twined tighter and tighter around her arms and legs. She concentrated, and when she did, her forces gathered and focused into a violent whirlwind that extinguished the blaze.

Serena pulled Jimena from the embers and smoke and knelt beside her.

Jimena was dying.

CHAPTER TWENTY-THREE

CATTY LEANED OVER HER. "Is she going to be okay?"

"I don't know." A hollow ache spread through Serena.

"Maybe if I take her back in time," Catty offered, her eyes wide as her pupils began to dilate.

"No," Serena whispered, but already the air had started to change as Catty readied for a trip back in time. Then Serena remembered the key. "Wait." She took it from her skirt pocket and placed it around Jimena's neck.

Catty knelt beside her. "What are you doing? I'll take her back to before she stepped into the fire and keep her from going in."

Serena shook her head. "It's too late for that."

Catty nodded. The air became still again. A tear rolled off her cheek and fell on Jimena's arm. "What will the key do?"

Serena held Jimena tightly. "I hope it will unlock the right door and bring her back."

A chorus of *ahhs* made them look up. Vanessa became completely invisible now. The show ended. Police officers pushed the crowd back behind the barricades. It was only minutes before paramedics would see Jimena and come running with their red metal cases. Serena knew intuitively that she couldn't let them take Jimena from her, not until Jimena found the door in the dark and used the key to unlock it and come back to the light.

"Look," Catty whispered.

Bluish arcs sparked around the key and then it vanished.

A moment passed, and then Jimena's eyes opened with a strange shudder.

"Hey." Jimena smiled weakly. "So I guess I showed you I'm still the tough goddess."

"You're bad, all right." Serena breathed out in relief. She squeezed Jimena. "I'm glad you made it back."

"Here they come," Catty warned.

Paramedics were running toward them.

"Let's get out of here," Serena said. "Can you stand?"

"If I made it through that, I guess I can stand," Jimena answered, but her legs were shaky and Serena had to help her up.

"Where's Vanessa?" Serena asked.

"She said she'd meet us back at the car." Catty grabbed Jimena's other arm.

Jimena, Catty, and Serena ran through the firefighters and news reporters to Jimena's car. Vanessa was waiting there, gasping for breath, her face red.

"You were great!" Catty said.

They scrambled into Jimena's car and she

started the engine. The tailpipes thundered as they pulled away from the curb.

"You sure were one bitch with an attitude," Jimena told Serena.

"I'm sorry." Serena felt that those words couldn't begin to make up for what her friends had done for her.

"I'm going to remember this forever," Catty announced. "You owe us big-time."

"I can't believe you took such a risk," Serena said to Jimena. "Going into the fire!"

"How 'bout Vanessa?" Catty added.

"Yeah." Serena turned and looked at Vanessa. "You were always afraid of having people see you go invisible."

Vanessa smiled triumphantly. "By tomorrow everyone will think it was an illusion caused by the fire and helicopter spotlights. No one would believe I actually became invisible."

"Not unless they're kissing you and see you go," Catty reminded her with a laugh.

"Vanessa's right," Jimena added. "Everyone will think it was some trick of the camera."

After a moment, Serena spoke slowly. "What was it like?"

"You mean when I was gone?" Jimena asked.

"Yeah, where did you go?" Catty was awestruck. "And how did you get back?"

"Hekate," Jimena mused. "She led me back. I had Serena's key, but she guided me to the right door."

Serena looked out the window. She was still feeling guilty.

Jimena glanced at her when she stopped at a red light. "You would have done the same for me," she said softly.

At home Collin was watching *Eyewitness News* on the television when Serena and Jimena walked in.

"What were you doing so near the methane gas explosion?" Collin asked.

"I've got to tell you the truth." Serena looked at Collin seriously. "I'm a goddess, and tonight I almost became the goddess of witches."

Collin stared at her oddly, then he broke into one of his great laughs and hugged her. "You've got the most bizarre imagination of anyone I've ever known, but that's part of what I love about you."

He let her go and turned to Jimena. "Are you a goddess, too?"

"Did you ever have any doubt?" Jimena bent her head to the side and gave him a sweet smile.

Serena loved the easy way Jimena could flirt.

"I guess I always knew." Collin shook his head. "So you two wanna make some popcorn and watch TV? There's a sci-fi marathon on tonight."

"Sure," Jimena said.

"Yeah, why not?" Serena looked from Jimena to Collin. She was happy they were finally getting along.

ON MONDAY, Serena saw Zahi in the hallway after school. He looked confused and embarrassed. He started to apologize.

"For what?" She touched his arm and looked into his eyes.

"Thank you," he finally said.

"You're welcome."

Zahi smiled tentatively and walked away.

Then Morgan strutted toward her, wearing tight black capris and a shiny snakeskin halter-top, the he-goat amulet proudly displayed on a thick gold chain. Serena had seen her running away with the other Followers the night of the cold fire and knew she was one of them now.

"I know what you did to him," Morgan accused in a nasty whisper. "But I'll get him back." She pinched the charm and dangled it in front of Serena in challenge.

"I won't let you," Serena warned.

Morgan gave her an arrogant smile. "It's official now, isn't it, Serena? Our clash is finally real."

"I never wanted to fight you, Morgan. You always started it with your attitude. I would have been your friend—"

"Right," Morgan sneered. "Try and stop me now." She turned with a snap of her heels and hurried down the hallway to Zahi.

"Morgan's one of them now," Jimena said flatly.

Serena turned, surprised that Jimena and Catty had been standing behind her. They looked at each other sadly.

"You think she'll bring Zahi back?" Catty looked anxious.

"Not with us around," Jimena said.

Serena shook her head. "I went into his

mind. I can't read his thoughts because it's all French and Arabic, but I wanted to see if I could feel anything. The Atrox is gone."

Morgan turned and gave Serena a wicked glare, then she walked backward, grinning at Serena in challenge. *Later,* her mind whispered before she turned and sauntered slowly away.

"What's up with Morgan now?" Vanessa asked as she joined them.

"She's a Follower," Jimena stated, her body tense with new anger.

Vanessa's face fell.

Serena clasped her shoulder. "We tried to protect her," Serena said.

"Yeah," Vanessa agreed and bit her lip.

"And you got Zahi back," Catty said to Serena "That was more important."

"We *all* got him back," Serena corrected.

Michael ran up to them, smiling. The air filled with his nice spice-soap smell.

"Hey." He slipped his arm around Vanessa and gave her a quick kiss. "What's up?"

"I'll see you guys tomorrow." Vanessa smiled

and walked off with Michael.

"I'm late." Catty looked at her watch. "I'm working for my mom this afternoon."

They waved good-bye and Jimena and Serena started walking down the hallway in the opposite direction.

"You wanna hang out?" Jimena asked.

"No, I got something I have to take care of," Serena said. "Will you feed Wally for me?"

"Sure. You need a ride where you're going?"

"No thanks. Got one."

Serena walked off campus and when she was sure no one was watching, she headed down a side street, then ran over to La Brea.

Stanton's car was parked in front of Pink's hot dog stand. Its sleek black metal reflected the late afternoon sun. He glanced up and smiled in recognition. He walked up to her and wrapped his arms tenderly around her. She pressed against him, enjoying his gentle touch. Then he kissed the top of her head and she looked up at him, her eyes now unguarded.

"Ready?"

Don't miss the next

DAUGHTERS OF THE MOON book,

night shade

J

IMENA STARTED ACROSS the dark kitchen when she saw someone going through one of the cupboards She grabbed a cast-iron skillet from the stove and turned on the light.

"Veto!" she gasped. The skillet fell to the floor with a loud thud.

Veto smiled lazily, his flashing eyes and high cheekbones as bold and beautiful as those of his Mayan ancestors.

She must still be dreaming. Veto had been dead a year now.

"Jimena." His whisper across the room filled the empty ache inside her. How many nights had she imagined seeing him again?

"What—" She started to ask him what had happened, but he closed her mouth with a kiss.

Her finger caressed the tiny scar that slashed his right cheek. His skin felt warm.

A noise startled her and she pulled away.

Her grandmother stepped into the kitchen. "Jimena, what was that noise? Were you talking to someone in here?"

"Veto," she started to say, but before the word left her mouth she turned back. The kitchen was empty.

She touched her lips remembering his kiss. Were her feelings for Veto still so strong that she had conjured up his ghost?